TOO SLOW ...

I had just turned when a voice from out the darkness said, "Say, mister, take a look at this guy, will you? I think he's been hurt."

I whirled around, stood for a moment listening, but could hear nothing—see nothing.

I moved slowly forward. As I went I dropped my hand to the .32 in my shoulder holster.

A guy's face loomed out of the darkness right in front of me. Too late, I saw it was Nick Pullen.

I whipped around, the .32 in my hand, but I wasn't quick enough. The guy behind me had had plenty of time to take aim with his blackjack.

Something exploded inside my head like a busted light globe.

Maybe I got slugged twice. I wouldn't know. Once was enough.

LARRY KENT, P.I.

CRY TWICE, KITTEN!

HONEY-BLONDE BLUES

DON HARING

A BOLD VENTURE PRESS BOOK

LARRY KENT 539
"Cry Twice, Kitten!"
by Don Haring
First Published by The Cleveland Publishing Pty Ltd.
Copyright © 2019 Piccadilly Publishing, All rights reserved.
First US Edition: December 2019

LARRY KENT 540:
"Honey-Blonde Blues"
by Don Haring
First Published by The Cleveland Publishing Pty Ltd.
Copyright © 2019 Piccadilly Publishing, All rights reserved.
First US Edition: December 2019

Names, characters and incidents in this book are fictional, and any resemblance to actual events, locales, organizations, or persons living or dead is purely coincidental.

All rights reserved. No part of this book may be reproduced or transmitted in any form or by any means, electronic or mechanical, including photocopying, recording or by any information or storage and retrieval system, without the written permission of the author, except where permitted by law.

This is a Bold Venture Press book

Series Editor: David Whitehead

Published by arrangement with Piccadilly Publishing

A BOLD VENTURE PRESS BOOK

CRY TWICE, KITTEN!

Jacob Troy was an old man who had it all; a moviestar wife, a vast and thriving business empire—even a castle he'd bought in Germany and had transplanted brick-by-brick onto some of Hollywood's primest real estate. But he wanted more. That's why he had hired mobster Danny Hester to put the squeeze on nightclub owner Paul Huntsman.

Huntsman hired Larry Kent to find a connection between Troy and Hester that would stand up in a court of law. If he could expose Troy, then he could ruin him.

Almost before Larry took the case, however, things moved fast. A case of kidnap, a sadistic beating, a neat little frame-up and a grisly murder, just for starters.

What should have been a straightforward assignment soon found Larry Kent fighting for his life.

1

How many dames make five?

"Take a look," said Callendar.

The big black Cadillac had pulled up smoothly on the clear space outside the Copacabana. There was the usual crowd gathered on the sidewalk to see the celebrities arrive; tourists mainly from out of State, and Hollywood residents just stopped by to take a look, and guys like myself, over in the Sunshine State because a guy must live.

A flunkey held open the door of the Cadillac and a dame stepped out.

I heard a little gasp of admiration from a couple of tourist dames in front of me.

"Genevieve Troy," said Vincent Callendar. "The girl who didn't need a press-agent to marry a millionaire."

She took a few steps away from the car, stopped and half-turned waiting.

"That's him," said Callendar.

A little, old, wizened-up guy like a tired monkey had clambered out the car, shaken off the hand the flunkey offered him and tottered after the gorgeous blonde who had preceded him. She was dressed in an ivory gown that fitted her like a sheath. Her golden blonde head was poised on a long, graceful neck and I saw, in the light pouring from the Copacabana entrance, the flash and glitter of diamonds, in her hair, at her throat, her ears, on her hands as she unpeeled long gloves. She seemed to be smiling and talking animatedly as the two of them made their way slowly to the doors. She seemed unaware of the small crowd that was watching her so intently, and so was he. He had his hand on her arm, and she towered over him like one of those statuesque amazons with a captive male in tow.

The crowd gave no demonstration. In fact, they were strangely silent as the two headed up the shallow steps. I guess it was just another entertainment to them—something to look at, like a flea-circus or a two-headed guy at a tennis match.

"Well?" said Callendar.

"Well what?"

"What did you think of her?"

I shrugged, lit a cigarette.

The crowd was dispersing. The doorman at the Copacabana had re-emerged, having piloted the couple inside. Another car pulled up, spilling out a couple of once-famous film stars. But the onlookers had lost interest.

We walked to the corner and Callendar tried vainly to flag down a cab.

I said, "How old is he?"

"Older than most of the mortgages around Beverly Hills."

"Okay," I said. "Why not just let him die? Then your client can move in on Jacob Troy's estate."

He gave me a fleeting smile. "I see you brought your Yankee sense of humor with you, Larry."

"Yeah," I said, "I also brought a man-size thirst."

"I'll do my best to help you over that one." He dived away from me as a taxi slowed a dozen yards away. He managed to grab it and as he got in, said, "Having seen the lady, maybe you've got some idea now what Huntsman is up against."

"I wouldn't have any idea," I told him. I dragged at my cigarette. "For my money, Hollywood's got more luscious blondes to the square acre than any other place on earth. So what does Genevieve Troy have?"

"She's got Jacob," replied Callendar tersely, and lapsed into a moody silence.

Vincent Callendar was a good lawyer. He was also a good guy who had made one big mistake in his life—he had gone over to California to practice law. Which meant he had suntan even on his ulcers.

He had called me long-distance and offered me a thousand dollars to help out a client, Paul Huntsman, who was in plenty trouble. Seems this Huntsman was a realtor with a big stake on the West Coast. At least he did have until the fabulous Jacob Troy moved in on him. Among other interests, Huntsman had the Santa Rosa Estate which he had converted into a plush roadhouse on the highway between Los Angeles and Santa Barbara. Guys like Huntsman get the urge now and then to give their dough a fancy cellophane wrap with tinsel and glitter to make it even better. Huntsman had put plenty dough into that roadhouse, but it was just too bad that Troy, with his usual methods of undercover finance manipulation, secretly bought out a weak member of Huntsman's syndicate and proceeded to eat into Huntsman's domain. Huntsman got wise to this too late—Troy was not the kind of guy you gave a head-start when you wanted to beat him in anything from a game of pinochle up.

And right then, in the middle of the fight between one financial big shot—Huntsman and Troy—a guy so big he had a grade all to himself—things got tough out at the Santa Rosa Roadhouse, and rumors of racketeering crept in.

That was when Huntsman's lawyer, Vincent Callendar, started to sweat nights. He figured that the way things were going Huntsman would wind up not only with a kitty sadly depleted but a bad name as well. He figured it was time he called in some guy who could do some undercover work with regard to Troy's connection with one, Danny Hester.

It looked like I was the guy.

This Danny Hester. His was a new name to me. Callendar had already told me Hester was regarded as a coming man, the youthful czar of a dozen flourishing rackets along the West Coast—including that of taking over control of the liquor supply to Huntsman's Santa Rosa club and a big percentage of the take from Huntsman's gaming tables.

"He could be on Jacob Troy's payroll," Callendar told me. "But I doubt it. Whenever Troy wants to employ undercover men, he picks on unknown guys. Big as he is he can't afford to have his name linked with anything downright shady."

I looked at him. "Are you kidding?"

"I never kid," said Callendar, "about guys who have as much power as Jacob Troy."

***

The bar had been designed to represent a Spanish galleon, with one wall painted like a brown sail and another bearing a mural depicting a lot of guys pulling oars like they weren't enjoying their work. The waiters were tricked out in costumes supposed to be those worn by Spanish sailors at the time galleons were around. They were plenty hot and uncomfortable.

I said, "How crazy can you get?"

Callendar shrugged. "This is Hollywood."

We sat on stools at the bar. The bartender looked normal enough except that he was wearing a tasseled cap with a skull and crossbones painted on the front.

"Scotch on the rocks," I told him.

Callendar had a martini.

When the bartender told me what the score was I nodded and said, "You're sure wearing the right hat, buddy."

He scowled at me and went his way.

We sipped our drinks.

Callendar said, "I'll have you talk with Huntsman tomorrow."

"Make it tonight," I told him. "I don't want to advertise my contacts in daylight. Say, how long has the blonde been Mrs. Troy?"

"About six months."

"What cradle did he snatch her out of?"

"She was in movies," said Callendar, a smooth dark guy who was getting too fat for his own good. He wore a look of worry on his pan like it belonged there. "Genevieve never quite made the big time, but with her stunning looks and that figure, she didn't lack for work. The story is she came to the coast after working as a model in some mid-western town." He shrugged. "What the hell. This is one place on the globe where it's almost impossible to find out where a dame started and how. You know how it is?" He bought more drinks. "The story is that Genevieve made a play for old Troy at some Convention. Sounds unlikely, because Troy's not the kind of guy goes to Conventions. However—she must have met him some place and there can be no doubt that she made a play for him, whatever the circumstances. So, in the words of the old song, they got married."

"Any folks?"

"Brother," said Callendar, "that guy must be eighty."

"I mean does Troy have any family?"

"Oh sure, there's quite a bunch of kin in the background. But Troy won't have anything to do with them. With all the dough he's got they stick around. His brother's Willard Troy, who made a lot of money twenty years back, supplying bum electric light tubes to movie studies—or some such. Whatever it was, he went broke the way he always has done. He lives out at Beverly Hills and I guess he just makes it—on his wits."

I was half-turned on my stool watching the guys and dames making to and fro.

"Brother Willard never married, but Jacob Troy's sister did. That's Mildred Delamore, who was married to A. K. Delamore." He paused expectantly.

I said, "So what?"

"I thought you wanted to know," he said in a pained voice. He took a sip of his drink then pulled a wry face. "One of these days I'm going to lay off this stuff. You know something, Larry, a guy's nuts to drink in this climate."

"Too tropical?" I hazarded.

He said, "You ought to remember A. K. Delamore. He was the guy floated a couple of the biggest movie productions ever—an independent. However, he started fooling around with real estate and that's when he ran into trouble." He took another sip. "One thing Jacob Troy doesn't like and that is guys moving in on his territories. He proceeded to make mincemeat out of his brother-in-law, A. K. Delamore. Delamore wound up running his car over a cliff at Lucinda Beach."

"Nice family."

"Yeah," said Callendar. "They don't come any ruggeder. Mildred's quite a dame. I met her two, three times. One of these tall, hard old bats, with a face like a rock and a heart dug out the same quarry. Her daughter's Angel Delamore."

I looked at him.

"Say," he complained. "You're way down on local history."

"Yeah," I said. "I never did get round to reading those movie handouts. I take it she's something in Hollywood?"

"Sure is," said Callendar with satisfaction. "Angel's a dish, a little peacherino! She's also an awfully bum actress, but I guess she'll get there just the same. Mildred has a son, too, the well-known Rod. He's a lush." He stopped talking and I saw a wary look close in on his pan.

I waited.

He went on, "You don't have to talk of the devil around here—it's always happening." He swung back to face the bar and murmured, "The Mouse just came in."

I saw a small, slender dame with orange-colored hair standing just inside the door. She was looking around expectantly.

I said, "One of these dyed mouses?"

"Her name's Dodo King," said Callendar staring at the drink in his hand. "She also happens to be Rod Delamore's doll."

"Does she act in movies, too?"

"She doesn't have to," said Callendar. "She was married once to a guy back in Pennsylvania and she peeled off a quarter-million in settlement when they divorced."

"Why, hello, Vincent," said a high clear voice right behind us.

We turned and there was the Mouse. She was smiling. "You guys gonna buy me a drink, or do I die of thirst right here in the middle of the desert?"

The Mouse was perched on the stool between us. She smiled at me.

Then she said to Callendar, "Who's the big, handsome boyfriend, Vincent?"

Callendar introduced us. Then he said, "If you'll excuse me just a moment I'll go and make a phone call."

I looked at him.

He said deliberately, "I better fix that appointment for you tonight,

Larry."

"Sure," I said. "You're excused."

He went away.

The Mouse ordered a gin and Indian tonic. I'd noticed that she was small; her eyes were big and baby-blue. She had a wide mouth and dimples. She had a trick of leaving her mouth open a little when she'd finished saying something, and resting the tip of her tongue on her lower lip, like she was all set to say something else, but couldn't quite make it.

I said, "Why the hair?"

"You like it?"

I shrugged. "It's different."

"That's the main thing," said the Mouse. "In this world, Mr. Larry Kent, you've just got to be different or you're dead."

I drank some more of my Scotch.

She wriggled a little closer to me. In a confiding whisper she said, "I hate having my hair this color really, but I guess my hairdresser talked me into it. You see, last month I was brunette but I was awful tired of that. It had always been sort of murky blonde before that, and when I went dark I used to scare myself every time I looked in the mirror."

I said, "How about now? Have you quit looking in mirrors?"

She laughed, staring at me. Then she said, "Cute."

"Yeah," I said. "Have yourself another drink."

"Oh, no, I want to keep stone-cold sober—for Rod."

"Uh-huh?"

"He's my boyfriend, and he should be here, but of course he isn't. He never is. Not when I want him. You know Rod Delamore?"

I shook my head, took out cigarettes.

She took one from my pack and I lighted it and then my own.

"Rod's sweet, a doll really, but he just doesn't know when to stop once he starts with that liquor."

"Tough."

"Specially for me," sighed the Mouse. Then her face brightened. "Maybe he's just caught in some crap-game some place."

"Sure," I said. "There's always a sunny side."

She looked at me. "Are you one of these wise guys?"

"No," I told her, "I'm just over here for my health."

She had some of her drink. The hard light shone on her orange hair. I said, "You been around Hollywood long?"

"Too long, I sometimes think. This place is dead after New York."

"Uh-huh."

"If it wasn't for Rod I guess I'd go someplace else, but—" She sighed again. "I think I might marry him, settle down and have a family." She shot me a sidelong glance. "How'm I doing, Larry?"

"Great," I told her. "You sure know the dialogue."

She laughed, showing a pink tongue. "You know, if Rod should come in he'd probably get jealous as hell."

"Too bad."

"But I guess it might do him good to get jealous once in a while. He sort of takes me for granted." For the first time a genuinely pensive look came into her eyes. Then she glanced down at her hands and said, "He's a heel, but he's all I've got."

I said to the bartender, "Another Scotch and another poisoned tonic-water."

We were halfway through it when a hand suddenly fell on my shoulder, all but thrusting me off the stool.

"Excuse me," said a voice thickly. "You're crowding my girl."

I looked up. He was big, he could have been well muscled only he didn't have any muscles any more. His face, his whole body, seemed to have spilled over as if the liquor had made him run over at the sides. He was young, but there were bags under his eyes like portmanteaus and his mouth was blubbery.

The Mouse was on her feet. She said, "Rod! What's the big idea coming in, pushing people around?"

"I'm pushing nobody," said Delamore. He looked at me. He added belligerently, "Am I punk?"

I said nothing.

The Mouse twittered. "You know you shouldn't do things like that. You don't know your own strength, Rod Delamore."

He snickered, then he stooped and kissed her on the bare shoulder. "Missed me, honey?"

"Please Rod—"

"Look, I'm sorry I'm late. I got kinda held up. I've got a table round at Delmonico's. We can go round right away and have ourselves some supper."

"Well, I don't know—"

"I do," said Delamore. "Say, is that your purse?" He reached out to the bar, but his hand didn't make it. I had his wrist clamped in my right hand.

He turned his head slowly and his mouth was a little open in surprise. He said thickly, "What you think you're doing, buddy? Committing suicide?"

I got off the stool, still holding his wrist. I said, "You don't know your own strength." I pulled him close to me, so the other customers wouldn't see me hit him. I hit him. It was a short one right into the belly.

He folded.

I pushed him away and he fell on his backside and then his head. He thumped on the tiled floor.

The Mouse gave a little scream, then quickly covered her mouth with her hand.

There was some excited talk and one of the waiters hurried over.

Back of me I heard the bartender say, "What happened?"

I looked at him. "He fell over," I told him. "He's drunk." I nodded to the Mouse. "See you around, baby."

Her blue eyes were wide. She said nothing. I went out.

I leaned against a car parked out front of the bar and Vincent Callendar came hurrying.

"I was looking for you—"

"Yeah," I said. "How did you make out?"

He waved a hand in the air. "Say, what happened in there? I heard a lot of talk—"

"Rod Delamore came in," I told him. "He was canned. He fell over."

He threw me a hard look. "Fell?"

"Yeah," I said. "How did you make out with Huntsman?"

"He'll see you right away. It's quite a drive, Larry."

"You got your auto in town?"

"Sure. Over at the lot."

"Let's go."

On the way out of town Callendar told me about Jacob Troy's place over at Burnt Springs.

"It's fabulous," he said, using a word that gets worked to death in Hollywood. "It's an old baronial castle he ran across when he was making a European tour some years back. He transported it stone by stone from the Rhine Valley and built it smack on top of a cliff overlooking the river. Back of him there's a lot of wooded country and he bought it all so he'd never have neighbors too close. A lot of tourists go to Burnt Springs but nobody gets past the gates leading to Troy's private road."

He spun the convertible round one of the steep bends. We were still climbing.

He went on, "It must be a crazy set-up. Just Troy and his ultra-glamorous wife, and about six servants, hand-picked of course. Around the grounds, I guess there are plenty of strong-arm guys prowling, German shepherd dogs, too, and burglar alarms rigged, in case anybody's crazy enough to get that close. Larry, how do you figure a guy like Troy makes out? I mean, when he's all alone nights, thinking about the guys he's busted, and the dough he's made?"

I said, "Maybe he plays gin rummy with his ultra-glamorous wife."

"You know, Larry," he complained. "You don't take this Troy serious enough."

I said, "Maybe Huntsman's taking him too seriously."

"You don't know the set-up," he warned. "But—you'll learn, that is if you live that long."

I said nothing for a moment, watching the white guide posts flick by in the powerful lights of the convertible. Then I said, "What's with this 'live that long' talk, Callendar?"

He laughed uncomfortably. "I didn't mean it quite like that."

"How do you mean it?"

"Look, would you light me a cigarette? I don't like to take my hands off the wheel."

I saw the needle was touching seventy. I said, "Keep your hands right there, buddy."

I lit two cigarettes together and handed one over to him, pushed it between his lips. He nodded, waggling the cigarette.

I said, "One thousand bucks underwrites my visits. The score as I got it was, that I was to look up certain contacts of Danny Hester's, and one in particular, Al Lardner, whom I knew back East years ago as No-Face."

"Well, Larry—"

I went on, "As I read it, I was to try and find out what contact, if any, there was between Hester and Jacob Troy, who is putting the squeeze on Huntsman. Correct me if I'm wrong, but is there anything in that assignment to make me double my life insurance?"

"Now, you don't have to take it that way," complained Callendar. He slowed and then shot past a heavy truck lumbering along with red sidelights showing. When he swung back on to his course he went on, "It isn't as if you're a stranger to risk, and after all, guys like Al Lardner don't play for peanuts." Again he laughed awkwardly. "Don't tell me you're scared, Larry. I just wouldn't believe that—"

I said, "Quit holding out on me, Callendar. You're one jump ahead and I don't like it."

He lifted his hand momentarily from the wheel, took out the cigarette and laid it in the tray above the dash. He said, "Well, I did use one guy from a detective agency in Los Angeles, but he kind of got off on the wrong foot with Hester and—well, Larry, the point is he must have had some sort of accident, this guy from the detective agency. They found his auto piled up and—well, maybe he'd been beaten up a little. I never did get around to clearing it up."

I said, "Maybe one of his wheels fell off, huh?"

"That's the way it is, Larry. I guess you won't want to change your mind now about doing this little bit of work for Huntsman?"

I said, "Quit fooling around, Callendar. You'd be surprised what I'd do for a thousand bucks."

The Santa Rosa was bigger than I'd expected—big and sprawling. There were a lot of lights spilling on to the short side road that led from the highway, and the parking lot was just about full.

"A lot of trade comes by here," said Callendar, as he locked the car. "Say, Larry, before we go in."

"Yeah?"

"About Huntsman. He's plenty bitter. He told me tonight he's got that way he suspects every second guy around Santa Rosa to be on Hester's payroll, undercover."

I leaned against the wing of the car and lit a fresh cigarette. I said patiently, "Okay, what does he want me to do?"

"Go in and have yourself a drink—we won't go in together. There are a couple of girls here, Huntsman told me, and they'll be waiting to kind of keep me busy while you're doing your stuff. After you've had your drink, go through to what Huntsman calls the Shell. You can have a whirl at the roulette wheel for a time and then some guy will come along and suggest you might like a quiet game of poker or some such. Go with him and he'll take you to Huntsman."

"Sounds plenty involved."

"That's the way Huntsman wants it."

"Okay," I said. "That's the way I want it, too." I nodded to him.

"Wait a minute."

I looked at him.

"I'll be in the cabaret with these two girls. I'll give you a half-hour then come back to the car. I'll drive away from this lot and wait for you just past the fork to the highway. You pick me up there, huh?"

"Half an hour? I guess that'll be enough."

I had nothing to check at the cloak room in the lush lobby. Back at the hotel I'd changed into a tuxedo before keeping my date with Vincent Callendar. Going through to the bar I checked on my cigarettes. I felt someone staring at me and turned to see a thin, sad-faced guy with a bald head and long, upper lip.

He moved toward me and said, "Can I help you out, sir?"

Very civil.

I said, "I'm a stranger around here. Where's the bar?"

"Right through there." He pointed. "Glad to have you at the Santa Rosa."

"Thanks."

"I'm Nick Pullen. We're always glad to have visitors out here."

I nodded to him and went through to the bar, bought myself a drink and turned to look around me.

It was a big layout. Huntsman sure had spent plenty of money on it. He even had some good murals on the walls and plenty mirrors, subdued lighting, expensive carpets, and—beyond the archway—a vast cabaret, stage and dance floor, tables crowded with late diners.

I finished my drink and nodded to the tight-lipped bartender and made my way through another archway. I paused a minute, looking about me. The guy who called himself Pullen was standing with his hands behind his back.

He nodded to me and said, "How you making out?"

"Where's the Shell?"

"Right through there, mister—what did you say the name was?"

"I didn't say." I looked at him. His face was inscrutable. I said, "I'm Larry Kent. I'm staying at the Sheridan Hotel in Los Angeles. What else you want to know?"

He was smiling faintly. He said, "That's all right, Mr. Kent. We just like to know who visits with us."

I said, "Must keep you kind of busy, checking on all those customers out there."

"We don't check on everybody, Mr. Kent, only on the ones we figure are important."

I said, "You got a good line there, brother."

"This way, Mr. Kent." He led the way through to a big room with vaulted ceiling. The lighting was brighter there, especially over the gaming tables. "Just help yourself. If you want chips, want to cash a check—there are people around to help you, Mr. Kent."

I said, "Where do I apply to have myself some luck?"

He laughed and I left him, made my way to the main roulette table and had myself fifty bucks on a number that got me fives. A good investment. I played it again and lost. The third time I doubled my stake and won. A hand touched my arm and I half turned. It was Nick Pullen.

"One moment, Mr. Kent."

I moved away from the table.

Pullen said, "You're wanted on the telephone."

"Uh-huh."

He turned and led the way out. Nobody seemed interested. We went through a padded pass door, down a short corridor and paused at a white-painted door.

"He's waiting for you, Mr. Kent."

As he moved away I turned the knob of the door and went in.

A guy sitting at the desk in the center of the room glanced up, got to his feet as I closed the door and leaned against it.

"Larry Kent?"

"That's right."

"Glad to have you here." He moved round the desk and held out his hand.

As I shook it, I said, "This cloak and dagger work must be giving you ulcers, Huntsman."

He smiled bleakly—a tall, good-looking guy in his late forties. He had sandy hair that was thinning a little and his face was the kind dames usually associate with after-shave lotion and he-men smoking briar pipes.

"Unfortunately I have to take precautions, Mr. Kent. I was warned that you'd arrived, and I guess by now Callendar is happily installed with a couple of my girls."

"Some guys get all the breaks," I told him. I went to get a cigarette out but he said, "Have one of mine." He moved over to the desk and opened a silver box and offered it to me.

I took a cigarette and a light from him. The desk was cluttered with papers, antique inkstand, a date pad, a small vase of flowers and a silver-framed photograph of some dame. I noticed he didn't smoke.

"I won't keep you long, as I don't think it's advisable." He talked in a clipped, authoritative way.

I reminded myself that he was a big shot—although he had dropped a lot of dough through the manipulations of an even bigger shot. I said, "How about this Nick Pullen?"

Huntsman nodded, "I guess he's about the only man I've got around here that I can trust. He's been with me a long time."

"Things bad, huh?"

"They couldn't be worse." He sighed and fell to tapping with his long fingernails on the desk top. He didn't ask me to sit down.

I leaned there, smoking.

"Callendar will keep in touch with you and tell you any latest developments. The main thing is I want you to try and get close to Danny Hester through this contact of yours. What's his name?"

"No-Face Lardner, he used to be called. I believe he's on Hester's payroll."

Huntsman put a disgusted look on his pan. "I never thought I'd have to dicker with a racketeer."

"Maybe it won't come to that, Huntsman. All depends how this thing breaks."

He looked at me curiously. "What do you intend to do?"

"Try and get close to Hester. At least try and get as much dope as I can on him. If I find there's any link between him and Troy, I guess I'll have earned my retainer."

"I only hope Callendar is paying you enough, Mr. Kent."

"I'll get by."

"Has he warned you it could be risky?"

"Sure." I shrugged. I made to ash my cigarette, found I couldn't quite make the ash tray and moved round the side of the desk. As I leaned over it, I said, "I want you to give Callendar a list of all the guys you've had working here in the past six months so I can con it. I'd also like details of your more recent dealings with Troy—" I broke off.

He said, "What's the matter?"

I said nothing. My hand felt a slight vibration on the desk top. I saw under the overhang a small oblong box had been screwed there. I touched it. It was warm.

Huntsman's voice came insistently, "What is it you're so interested in there?"

I straightened. I saw a mess of wires leading to the four telephones on his table. I identified each one, then picked up a fifth, and it seemed to wind up right in back of one of the phones where the framed portrait stood. I reached out and picked it up. There was a tiny table microphone there.

I looked at Huntsman. "You always keep a record of your visitors' conversation?"

He stared at me, then at the thing in my hand. His face suddenly went red and he leapt forward. He said thickly, "Let me see that thing."

"Take it easy," I told him. "You mean you didn't install this gazebo?"

"Damned sure I didn't!" He seemed to be having trouble with his breathing. "Now see here, Kent—"

I said, "Choke it off." I reached down and got the end of the wire where it was fed into the recorder clamped under the table. I snapped it clear, then reached for my pocket knife, opened the blade and started working on the screws that held the recorder to the desk top. When I was through I held it up for Huntsman to see.

He stared at it for a moment in silence and then, "It must have been put there when I was through talking with the girls—"

"It wouldn't take long to install," I told him. I picked up the microphone and looked at it again. "I guess the wire spool on the recorder went into action the moment any sound waves hit the mike, and cut off automatically when the sound waves stopped."

"Some damned blackguard spy—" began Huntsman, but I checked him.

"This typical of the set-up?"

"They've never gone this far!"

I said, "Somebody knew I was coming. Somebody must have tapped your phone and then installed this gimmick. Looks like they've got you well-taped, Huntsman."

He suddenly went to his chair back of the desk and flopped into it. He said woodenly, "I feel licked," and then with his voice trembling with anger he added, "That damned Jacob Troy. He'd stop at nothing, nothing to break me. He thinks he'll smash me the way he did that brother-in-law of his, Delamore." He leapt to his feet. "Well, he won't win out. I'll kill him first!"

I said, "Slow down. For all you know there might be more microphones planted in the walls."

He whipped round at once and I said, "For Pete's sake, sit down, Huntsman."

He sat as if his legs were suddenly weak.

I lit a fresh cigarette from the silver box. I said, "Nick Pullen. Get him."

Obediently he put out a hand and pressed an alarm bell.

The door opened quietly and a guy stood there with an expressionless waiter's face.

"Get Nick."

"Sure, Mr. Huntsman." The guy was gone.

I dragged on my cigarette, looking at Huntsman. I said, "What triggered this feud with you and Troy?"

"I have no idea."

"Not good enough, Huntsman. He must feel plenty bad about you to not only want to beat you in business, but smash you as well."

"I've no idea why he feels that way."

"Maybe you're crossed him up in some deal years back?"

"Never."

"Maybe it's a more personal matter?" I waited.

Nothing came.

"You ever met Mrs. Troy?"

He looked at me sharply. I saw his face redden. He licked his lips. "As a matter of fact, I did know Genevieve a couple of years back. She was trying to break into movies."

"Uh-huh?"

"Don't get the wrong idea, Kent."

"I'm getting no ideas," I told him. "Maybe Troy's allergic to guys who had anything to do with his wife even before she married him."

"He's a crazy, jealous fool," blurted Huntsman. He bunched his big fist and crashed it on the desk top. "Once I get proof that he's playing along with that racketeer—that Danny Hester, I'll break him. I'll smear his name on every newspaper in the country. I'll—" He broke off.

The guy was back again.

"Well?" he barked.

The guy said, "Nick ain't around, Mr. Huntsman."

"What do you mean, not around? He was here a few minutes back!"

"He ain't here no more," said the guy. "Somebody said he went out."

I looked at Huntsman.

Huntsman said, "All right, Charlie, that'll do."

The door closed again.

I said, "Looks like Nick Pullen's clairvoyant!"

"I don't understand it," said Huntsman. He got to his feet and stood there, his face sweating a little.

I mashed out my cigarette. I stooped again to where the recorder had been clamped and looked more closely at a lead I had taken to be a cable to the switchbox for the telephones, but I saw that it ran away from the desk at a tangent, hitting the wall and disappearing there. I went over to the wall, stooped and stared at the minute pile of sawdust on the carpet.

As I straightened I said, "Pullen was getting it two ways. Recording our talk and listening at the same time."

Huntsman was at my side immediately. "What on earth's this? A telephone?"

I shook my head. "Somebody drilled that hole in the wall quite recently. What's on the other side of the wall?"

"My secretary's office. She's here earlier in the evening—"

"Not there now, huh?"

"There's nobody there to my knowledge."

"Let's go see." I crossed to the door and he followed me. He indicated the door down the passage and I went in. The room was in darkness. I snapped on lights. It was the usual office set-up with steel furniture and the only feminine touch a small vase of flowers, wilting a little after a long day. I went to the wall that communicated with Huntsman's office. I saw where the lead came out through the hole, and there was a single ear-piece attached to a tiny speaker. It had been left on the floor as if someone had discarded it in a hurry. I looked at Huntsman, who was glowering down at the gadget.

I said, "Pullen sneaked in here to have a listen. He knew the recorder would do the work for him, but when I cut off the current, he must have got wise and taken a powder."

"It mightn't have been Pullen," broke in Huntsman. His eyes looked mad. "Why I've known Nick Pullen for years and years—"

"Some guys can be bought," I pointed out. I dusted my fingers together. "You better get rid of this junk and—how about you take a trip to Florida, Huntsman?"

"What do you mean?"

"It's getting that way the boys are crowding you. If Pullen was standing this side of the wall tonight, he heard what we said. That means he's wise to me and I guess my value can be cancelled out as of now. But I intend to push it just the same."

"And I don't intend to quit," he told me. "I'm not going to Florida or any other place. I'm staying right here. No cheap racketeer is going to push me around—"

I said, "Huntsman, has it struck you maybe Hester's working independently of Troy?"

"I wouldn't believe that," he snapped. "Troy is out to get me and he's using Hester's set-up because he knows Hester's got the kind of guy who'll pull anything, go anywhere. And don't forget Hester has bought into concessions that supply this roadhouse, unknown to me of course until it was too late. I tell you, Hester's working for Troy—"

I said, "You've got no proof of that."

He shook his head angrily.

"It's up to you to find it."

"I can try. But if Pullen's taking Hester's pay, I'll sure be plucking air." I glanced around the office. "This could be a valuable set-up for a big-time gambler and racketeer like Hester. How about if he's throwing scares into you and putting on the squeeze just so he can take over himself?"

"I won't believe that," said Huntsman stubbornly. "Troy's back of all my troubles, the same as he has been for the last eighteen months."

"Okay," I said. "Have it your way. You contact me through Callendar, huh?"

I went out, down the corridor, through the Shell, back to the bar, where I had myself a Scotch.

Outside, the air was fresh with a hint of salt in it, and I remembered that the Pacific was not far away. I walked briskly across the grass that edged the circling drive-in. There were still cars rolling up toward the lot, and a few more leaving. I knew it was well over Callendar's half-hour, but I figured he'd wait. It was very dark away from the floodlit lot.

I had just turned on to the highway when a voice from out the darkness said, "Say, mister, take a look at this guy, will you? I think he's been hurt."

I whirled around, stood for a moment listening, but could hear nothing—see nothing.

I moved slowly forward. As I went I dropped my hand to the .32 in my shoulder holster.

A guy's face loomed out of the darkness right in front of me. Too late, I saw it was Nick Pullen.

I whipped around, the .32 in my hand, but I wasn't quick enough. The guy behind me had had plenty of time to take aim with his blackjack.

Something exploded inside my head like a busted light globe.

Maybe I got slugged twice. I wouldn't know. Once was enough.

2

Baby, take a walk ...

"Let's take a look at him," said a voice. Hands dragged me upwards. My head was booming but I found I could stand. They led me round the front of the car.

"Make him kneel down," said the voice.

They forced me down on my knees in front of the lights. One beam caught me squarely and I blinked. Pain was shooting through my head and the inside of my mouth was dry.

"Okay," said the voice. "I got a good look. It's him. Put him in back."

They hauled me up and walked me across over gravel. I shook my head. I could see the long, bulky outline of a trailer hitched to the back of the car and the door was swung open. They hustled me up the steps and threw me inside. I sprawled on the floor and heard the door slam and the door lock snapping. Then as I started to get to my feet, the towing car started up and the trailer pitched and swayed for a moment, then settled down to a steady run as we hit the concrete pavement.

Two small bulkhead lights showed me that I was in a section of the trailer furnished out like the cabin of a luxury cruiser. I hung on to the side of the table that was clamped to the floor and looked about me. The davenport was small, with brightly colored cushions scattered on it. There were even flowers and a wall plaque, a framed seascape on another wall.

I groped my way through to the next room, found there was a stateroom with double bunks in it, and beyond that a shower recess. Beyond that again was a miniature kitchen that seemed to be tricked out complete with everything.

I made my way back to what could be called the living room. I seemed to have the trailer to myself. I sat on the edge of the davenport and rubbed my hands through my hair. They hadn't broken the skin but I had a bump on the back of my skull like a pigeon's egg. I ran my tongue round my gums and I figured I was wasting time.

I got to my feet again, staggered to the closet in the corner. Sure enough there was liquor there. I took out a bottle of bourbon, broke open the top and tipped it to my teeth. It felt pretty good as it coursed its way down.

I replaced the bottle, closed the closet door and went through to the shower annex, ran the faucet over the hand basin, let the cold water pour over my face and neck. Then I dried myself off with a towel, went right back of that trailer to see if I could force one of the scuttles.

Everything seemed to be sealed up as tight as an attorney's mouth. It wasn't so cockeyed leaving me run around free that way.

The next minute the trailer was bouncing to a stop. I heard the door snap back. I strolled through to meet them, hands in the pockets of my tuxedo.

"Okay," said the voice I'd heard before. "Close the door."

As the door closed the guy said, "I'm Danny Hester. Be my guest."

There were three of them. They made me sit down on the davenport, and I leaned one elbow on the nearby table and smoked the cigarette they'd given me.

Danny Hester was sitting in the easy chair opposite me. He was younger than I figured he would be with a rugged pan, a deep cleft in his chin, and a firm rat-trap mouth. His eyes were brown, and in any other guy you would have called them clear and honest. He had brown hair, crew cut, and his ears were small without lobes to them, the way the experts say a murderer's are. He filled his imported tweed sports jacket without any benefit of padding. His tie was quiet and the brogues he wore over Argyle socks were of good make.

"What you figure is the payoff, Kent? A slug in the guts, maybe?"

The other two guys I felt I'd known all my life. One of them was Nick Pullen, the man who had double-crossed Paul Huntsman. The other was No-Face.

Al Lardner had got that handle way back in the times when Honegger was peddling hot liquor from Canada across into Michigan. They always figured Lardner was one guy who always held an alibi no matter what. When the cops ran him in a line-up, they were always mixing him up with two, three other guys. That way he skipped a lot of prison sentences. The truth was, Lardner was one con who used disguise; he was no slouch at it; he could put on a pair of spectacles and look a totally different guy; he could put wax inside his mouth and up his nostrils and look like somebody else again.

No kidding.

The cops knew it, of course. The trouble was the only way they could keep tabs on him was by fingerprints and even then he tried to fool them by having his finger-ends pared by a guy who'd been a surgeon in the U.S. Navy before they fired him for killing a guy.

That was No-Face Lardner. Years back he'd been a legend, but it'd been a long time since the cops had puzzled over his "mug portraits" or tried to tie in with some crime in which he swore he'd had no hand.

I figured he must have lost himself over in the West, maybe gone straight for a time before tying in with Danny Hester and his up-and-coming rackets.

"No talk," said Danny Hester. "Feed him another liquor, Nick."

Nick Pullen pushed himself off the wall. There was a mean gleam in his eye as he went to the table close to me, poured liquor and pushed it my way.

"Take it, take it," said Hester.

I nodded and drank. I put down the empty glass. Hester said pleasantly, "Now bust him one." Nick drew back his bunched fist.

Hester said, "You better hold him, Al."

Lardner laughed. He moved to the side of the davenport, reached out suddenly and grabbed me by the ears.

I ducked my head a little at the last minute, but Nick's knuckles caught me on the top of the head, bringing on that booming sound again.

Hester said, "Okay, let him relax a little." Then as they drew away from me, "Having fun?"

"Yeah," I said. "How are you making out, chiseller?"

Hester got to his feet. He rubbed his hands together, the flat palms making a rasping noise.

"You know," he said, "you're one guy I've been wanting to meet in a long time. Then what happens? You come over here to try and snoop into my racket and walk right into my parlor. A guy can be lucky at that."

"Sure," I said. "Only don't push it too far, Hester. Looks like the sands are running out."

He laughed. "You've crazy." He walked up to me. "Okay, on your feet."

I sat where I was.

"Stand up," he snarled and reached out and grabbed me by the tie and twisted it.

I got up slowly.

He knew I was setting myself for a punch. He threw me back suddenly so I bounced against the wall, slid back down to the davenport.

"This guy's mean," he said. His eyes were watchful. "Okay, Kent. Huntsman paid you to come out here, didn't he?"

"Sure," I said. "You've got the evidence. This two-timing Pullen put you wise."

As if I hadn't spoken he said, "Huntsman and that fancy lawyer of his, Callendar. They figure they can put the finger on me, don't they?"

I shrugged.

"Don't they, Kent?"

I reached out my hand for the cigarette pack and instantly Hester slapped my knuckles hard with the side of his palm.

I let my hand fall.

"Talk up," he said, "or I'll maul you before you get yours."

"If that's the way it's going to be," I told him, "go right ahead. If I'm going to wind up stiff, I might as well go out quiet."

"You won't be quiet before we're through with you," said Hester. He showed his teeth and I saw they were strong, even teeth that filled his mouth. "How long you been here?"

I said, "Day, two days, maybe. I lost count of time."

"You start counting it right away, big boy." He leaned his face close to mine. "We've messed you up a little tonight. It's nothing to what I'm gonna do to you later. Okay, boys, you stay with him. If he gets nervous, slug him."

Al Lardner said familiarly, "What you aimin' to do, Danny?"

"Use the radio telephone if it's any of your business."

He was at the door when Nick Pullen said complainingly, "I want to talk to you, Danny. With this guy lousing things up I won't be able to go back to the Santa Rosa—"

He broke off as Hester turned slowly to face him. Hester said, "You beefing to me with your troubles?"

"I only said—"

"Don't say. Just stick around here and do like your told."

"Okay, okay," said Pullen. "Only don't forget I put you wise to this bum shamus." Again he broke off.

Hester moved close to him. He said, "You putting me under an obligation, rat?" He whipped up his hand and backhanded Pullen across the mouth.

Pullen fell back with a muffled cry and Hester said, "You crossed up Huntsman. You'd do the same to me, only you won't get the chance." He jumped down the steps. I heard him crunch over the ground toward the car.

No-Face was looking at me. He was leaning against the wall, his arms folded. There was a faint grin on his mobile mouth.

I said, "Where you been all this time, No-Face?"

"Around." He shrugged.

"Working legit?"

"Why not? I got a job in the movies for a time. Stunt man. They did some mugs of me, too, until the cops got wise and wanted to freight me out of California on an extradition ticket." He laughed softly, but only the muscles of his cheeks moved. "They've got no hope in hell of takin' me any place."

Nick Pullen said from near the doorway, "That Danny Hester's mean tonight, Al."

Without turning his head, No-Face said, "Play it quiet, Nick boy. You don't know the half of Danny yet."

I said, "Okay if I smoke?"

"Sure, sure, go right ahead. Here, let me light it for you." He reached over and as I put the cigarette between my lips he snapped a lighter into action and suddenly rammed it against my cheek.

I whipped back and as he laughed I snapped up my brogue and caught him squared in the groin. He fell over me, his breath coming out in a tearing whistle of pain. He was right across me. I could feel the gun against me. I grabbed him hard, slammed him back on the davenport and dived for his gun.

Nick Pullen must have fired right away. The bullet screamed past my head and tore out through the bondwood wall of the trailer into the night.

"Drop it," snarled Pullen. "Drop it or you're dead!"

I eased myself back slowly.

Al Lardner wriggled himself from under me. He staggered over to the wall, holding himself, making retching noises; and then with a rush Danny Hester was back.

He hung there in the doorway, his face asking a question.

Without turning his head Nick Pullen said, "He got at Al. He was trying to get Al's gun when I fired at him. I figured you didn't want him killed, Danny, so I let the shot go wild."

"Good boy, good boy," said Danny approvingly. He walked right up to me and stared into my face. "You're mean," he said conversationally. He whipped up his hand and bounced his palm across the bridge of my nose, then he grabbed at my shirt front and hauled me upright. He held me close and said, "Too bad I can't really break you up. I've got a change of thought about you. You're going on a little ride, a one-way ride, and I don't want no more marks on you. None that will show!"

They left Nick Pullen in the trailer with me for the last ride. The whole time he had sat in the chair opposite the davenport, watching me, his gun on his lap.

Me, I lay back on the davenport and smoked cigarettes and wondered how the Mouse was making out. I didn't know why I was thinking about her—Dodo King with the orange hair and the alcoholic boyfriend. Some place, maybe, Rod Delamore fitted into the Jacob Troy affair—but Troy and his blonde wife and his sister Mildred and brother Willard and all the tribe—seemed a million miles away from that smoothly rolling trailer, taking me out on a one-way ride.

We stopped once and I heard voices. Some guy laughed.

I heard a voice say, "This is the first time a trailer went through this gate, Danny." Then we started up again and drove some way.

I knew we crossed a bridge, heard the slight rumble, the sudden dip as if we had left the planking, and then we swung hard over and ran smoothly over soft ground, there was a bump or two and then we stopped. There was silence.

Nick Pullen was on his feet. He was plenty alert after his run-in with me and Danny Hester's subsequent praise. Keen and alert he stood to one side as the door was plucked open and Danny Hester stood there.

"Get him out quick!"

Nick came over to me, rammed the gun against my head. "On your feet."

I got up and strolled to the door, paused for a moment, looked at Hester. He was down on the step, below my height.

Hester said, "Either here or inside, you can take your pick. Go quietly and you'll last a few minutes longer."

"My worries," I told him. I swung a low one at him and felt the sweet satisfaction of feeling my fist bounce deep into his guts.

He pitched headlong down the step and I leapt after him, stooped, diving for his throat.

I should have taken care of the other guys first. It must have been No-Face Lardner, evening the score, who slugged me with his gun barrel across the nape of the neck. I pitched sideways beside Danny Hester. I didn't go right out to it, but that booming in my head had got that way it was almost permanent.

There was a bit of confusion then. It was very dark out there. I could see a light way through the trees. It seemed to be high up, and when I looked closer I realized it was a very tall house. There seemed to be battlements, ornamentation, white masonry pointing, buttresses. Then there was an open door, small, set in a side wall unobtrusively. I was being hustled in and I heard Danny Hester in a low voice say, "Back to the trailer, Nick. You, Al, keep your gun on Kent. Walk him down real slow and then wait at the door."

Danny Hester disappeared.

"Walk," said No-Face softly.

I went down the narrow corridor and there seemed to be nothing on the walls or floor. It reminded me of a secret passage in a baronial castle that I saw when I visited Europe one time.

The thought made a bell ring in my head. I remembered Jacob Troy and the house he had transported stone by stone from the Continent. Could it be possible …?

We were standing at another door, waiting, and then the door opened and a flood of light came out.

"Right in here," came Danny Hester's voice, low pitched, urgent.

With the gun at my back I stumbled into the light, then stopped.

A few paces away across a deep pile carpet a dame stood—tall, statuesque, her white hands folded demurely in front of her. Her blonde head was held high on her long neck. There was a faint smile playing about her lips.

Genevieve Troy.

"Get him through to the other room," said Danny. "You keep him there, Genevieve."

She said nothing, but that faint smile was still on her face. She crossed to a door on the other side of the room, opened it and looked out. Then she beckoned to me.

I didn't move right away, but the gun was jabbed against my spine. I went across the room and through the door. Genevieve closed it behind me. I looked at her.

She said in a husky voice, "Don't try any tricks. Big brother's watching."

3

Holes in several heads ...

It was a small room, furnished sparsely. It reminded me of the anteroom to some big shot's office, except that instead of a reception desk there was a small table with a bowl of flowers on it and an indoor vine trailed across one wall. There were two chairs, a scatter rug, an old fashioned oil painting on one wall and that was about all. There was another door opposite the one through which we had entered. There were no windows. A single light shielded by a bowl shone from the ceiling.

"How does big brother come into the act?" I asked her. She went on smiling.

"I was speaking metaphorically."

I said, "Where did you get around to learning big words?"

The smile went. "I've been around," she said. Then added, "There's somebody right outside that door. You try anything fancy and see what happens to you."

I said, "You're scaring me to death." I leaned against the small table and folded my arms across my chest.

She was standing in the center of the small room, obviously waiting.

I said, "Looks like Danny Hester's got the run of this joint."

She made no answer.

"Guards on the gate fixed. Knows the ways in and out. Maybe Jacob Troy gave him a latchkey, too."

She looked at me. There was no expression in her eyes. "You can figure as much as you like, Larry Kent, you'll get no place."

She studied me. Something seemed to strike her suddenly, "How did you get this way? I mean—sticking your nose into other people's affairs and getting it cut off along with your head?"

I said, "I'm a reformer. I'm cleaning up the rackets, starting with big shots who marry the first dumb blonde they fall over."

I was trying to get her mad but it was like hacking at Mount Everest with an ice-pick.

She said, "Keep right on talking. It's good for my nerves."

"You got any?"

"Why not?" She laughed silently, then took a step toward me and stopped. "You know, if you'd been smart, you could've got some place, Larry Kent."

"Uh-huh?"

"You're a big, strong boy and I guess you've got some brain tucked away in back of that rugged exterior. I could have used a guy like you."

"I'm open to offers," I told her. I figured I was so far along the line it didn't matter; I was like that drowning guy clutching at soggy straws. "Just what you got in mind, baby?"

"I don't like being called baby," she snapped. She moved a little closer.

Now I could get the full impact—and brother it was plenty. She wore a perfume that was as subtle as the house gown that clung to her seductively. Her skin was very white and I could see faint blue veins at her temples. She was a big girl—all over.

"It's too late to make deals with me, Larry Kent. You pushed it too far. Besides, you made Danny mad."

"That's too bad. Does he make Jacob mad, too?"

She hauled off and cracked me. The slap made a sound like a pistol shot.

I said, "Easy. You might wake the baby."

I could see she was quivering with rage.

"Relax," I told her. "Why should you worry? You're sitting on twenty million bucks and you've got a racketeer boyfriend thrown in. What more you want? The Golden Gloves?"

I thought she was going to hit me again but she let her hand fall to her side. She even managed a smile, a sour one. "You're quite a guy, Larry Kent, and you've got quite a line. Too bad I didn't meet you a long time back. I'd have got a kick out of making love to you—and whipping you into line!" She spat out the last words.

I reached out and grabbed her by the upper arms.

She stood very still.

I said, "I go for the loving part, but no dame ever whipped me and got away with it."

"You're very sure of yourself, aren't you?"

"Why not?"

She had her head back a little. She was trying to look cold and distant and dignified and not making out. I could feel her skin trembling a little beneath the shimmering house gown under my fingers.

I said, "You're quite a dame." I pulled her close to me. It wasn't hard. She swayed all the way there to meet me. Her lips were parted a little, her eyes half-closed. I kissed her. Right then I got another of those explosives in the head—only for once I was liking it.

Suddenly she tore herself back from me. She gasped, "You great lug. You think you can buy me over—"

"Did I mention dough?"

"Oh, I know your kind—"

"You know hell," I told her. I grabbed her again and she fought against me for a moment then sagged weakly against my chest. I could feel her panting.

At last she said, "Larry—Larry, this is crazy—you've got to get out of here—"

"Sure. Which way? The far door?"

She lifted her head sharply. "That way? No, you fool—" She broke off. I could see her throat working—almost see the thoughts racing in her mind.

I said, "The way we come in is loaded. Where's the exit, Genevieve honey?"

"Call me that again and I'll carry you out myself."

We stared at each other for what seemed a long time, then she said, "Of course you're taking me for a ride. You're just using me—"

"You're nuts. You're the big bomb. You're what strong guys cry for. As if you didn't know." I added, "Genevieve honey."

She attempted a smile, failed. She was trembling like a teenager being kissed for the first time. And then three sharp knocks sounded on the door back of us.

She jumped away from me so fast she almost tripped.

I leaned back against the table.

The door opened cautiously. Danny Hester was poking his head in. He said nothing for a moment, looked at her and then at me. Then he moved right into the room, drew close to her and said, "What's eating you?"

"Danny—Danny, I can't go through with this."

I couldn't see the expression on his face but I could guess just what he was registering. He said nothing for a moment and then, "Time's run out, Jenny. Everything's fixed. Beat it."

She drew herself up. She said evenly, "Danny, you can't push me around."

"This is one time I do, baby. Get out there fast."

For a moment I thought she was going to buck him, but then without looking at me she sailed out the door.

Danny Hester turned slowly and there was a hard smile on the corners of his mouth.

"Making time, Kent?"

I said nothing.

"You should've told her goodbye." The smile had become a cruel one. "You won't be seeing her again, lover-boy."

He had a squat automatic in his hand. He jerked it at the far door. "Move over there fast."

I moved. I stood near the door. I waited. Nothing happened. I started to turn my head to say something to Hester and the next instant heard the sound of a shot.

It was muffled by the masking door but it was a shot, all right.

I turned then and looked at Hester. He was nodding slowly. He went right on waiting for maybe a minute longer, then he pushed past me, threw open the door and stood just inside the doorway, with his gun held smack against my stomach. His head was flung round so he could see right into the other room.

Tersely he said, "Okay, get in there."

I didn't get it.

I didn't get it even when I moved past him, the gun still covering me. Then I found myself in a much larger room with maybe a half dozen Persian scatter rugs littered about the flagstone floor. I had time only to see one dim light showing in the wall above the great line of books ... maybe they were dummies because Jacob Troy was not much of a hand at reading: except stock report. I had a sensation of spaciousness and mustiness; the sort of smell that hangs around a rich guy who's mean; a big guy who's shriveled up like a monkey and who has to buy his wives with mink and diamonds and all the things other guys would use to get wives if they had the loot.

And then I was alone.

Or it seemed I was alone. I hadn't heard the door close but Danny Hester was no longer with me. I stood very still for a moment and then heard a sound and whirled round.

Jacob Troy was lying beside a huge mahogany desk. He was lying on the floor. Both hands were stretched toward me as if he were grabbing at something. But I could see a part of his face and knew that he wouldn't be grabbing anything anymore.

But it wasn't Troy who had made the sound.

No-Face Lardner was standing a little to one side of him. For once there was a genuine expression on his smooth actor's pan—a look of unholy glee.

And then I got it. I took off like I was on a springboard making with a long dive. There was a squat chair set a few feet away, and it was that I headed for, low down, leaping.

I almost made it. I didn't hear Lardner's gun exploding. I didn't feel anything. He must have fired as I took off, and the bullet churned a parting in my hair and knocked me cold.

I must have been conscious, but it was a borderline waking, like being in the middle of a nightmare and trying to wake because you're aware that you are in a nightmare and you're fighting to wake.

I knew I'd been hit but I was alive. There must have been quite a lot of blood. My head wasn't aching so much as vibrating on a high note, like a plucked guitar string. And I was flat on my back. Under my right hand was a gun. I moved my hand away from it.

There were voices, urgent voices. I didn't have to open my eyes to identify them; Genevieve and the boyfriend, Danny Hester.

I heard Genevieve say, "Hubbard's out there calling—he must have been out of his room—heard the shot."

"To hell with that damn butler," said Hester roughly. "Al—you dropped the gun beside him?"

"Sure, boss."

"Then let's get the hell out of here."

"Danny!" Genevieve's voice became a wail. "You can't just quit, leave me like this—"

"You know what to do. Take it easy can't you—"

And then I could hear another voice, a strange one, from a long way off calling, "Mrs. Troy. Mrs. Troy."

"He'll be here any minute," said Hester. "And maybe the rest of the house staff with him. We got to scram, Lardner. I'll call you, baby."

"You can't do this to me—"

Then Hester's snarled reply, "Pull yourself together, can't you. Get out there and make with the big grief for Hubbard. We'll go out the side door. See you."

There was silence for what seemed like a couple of minutes.

Cautiously I opened one eye and then the other. From where I lay I couldn't see Jacob Troy's body but I knew it wasn't far away. I couldn't see anything that interested me all that much. I knew I was alive and I was glad of that, but from there on I had no great interest in anything.

I knew Genevieve Troy had left the room silently, maybe speeding out to put on her act with Hubbard, the butler. And then there came the sound of hurried footsteps. A door banged some place, deep in the house. There were excited voices. Somebody started howling, and a man's voice—I took to be Hubbard's—snapped, "Get that girl out of here, Mrs. Mosely," and then, "Mrs. Troy, this is terrible."

Genevieve's voice came tight and straight, "I daren't—I can't look again. I just can't bring myself to it."

"You wait in the other room, Mrs. Troy. I'll call the police. I'll fix everything."

"You'd better—get Coburn, hadn't you?"

"The lawyer?" Hubbard's voice sounded surprised. "I hardly think so at this stage, Mrs. Troy."

"Never mind. Just get the police and doctor."

"Sure, Mrs. Troy. You leave it with me. I'll use Mr. Troy's desk phone."

Genevieve said, "The other one—the man who must have killed him—is he dead?"

Curtly Hubbard's voice came, "I guess so, by the look of his head. All that blood."

"I thought I saw his hand move just now—"

"Please, ma'am, you must get out of here." He raised his voice and called, "Mrs. Mosely? Mrs. Mosely come here at once and see to your mistress."

There was some coming and going and through it I could hear Hubbard dialing the phone, a pause and then, "Police? This is Hubbard, butler at Mr. Jacob Troy's residence, Burnt Springs. There's been trouble out here. I'm afraid Mr. Troy is dead. What's that. Yes, I heard a shot and came down here and found a stranger in the library with Mr. Troy. They both seem dead—"

While he was talking I raised my head and managed to sit upright. I had to hold my head down for a little time to clear it, and then I got to my feet and staggered over to the wall. I leaned against it.

I heard the clatter of the phone as it was dropped toward the rest but missed it. I had my handkerchief out and was wiping down my face. I saw a big fat guy, with moon face, shaking like a jelly, standing over by the desk. Both hands were held out like a stage butler's caught in the act of pilfering the master's port.

I said, "They sending a doctor, too?"

His chin moved up and down but no sound came. His eyes were glazed over like a dead cod's.

And then there came a rush of feet. Genevieve Troy hurtled into the room and stopped, swung round to face me and screamed.

"Yeah," I said. "I guess I need a wash up. Maybe you can show me some place."

Slowly she took her hands from her mouth. Her eyes were big, staring. She stammered out, "Larry," and the next instant recovered herself and said, "You're Larry Kent. I've seen your picture."

"Yeah," I said, "I bet you have."

Then the butler moved into action. He came yammering across the room. "I thought this man was dead, Mrs. Troy, and he got up right there while I was calling the cops. I never had such a fright in my life—"

"Pipe down," I told him. "Where do I wash?"

As if habit was reasserting itself, he raised a trembling hand and pointed toward a narrow doorway in one corner of the vast room.

I nodded, walked over toward it and was almost there when Genevieve called, "Don't let him walk around, Hubbard. He's a murderer. A killer! Didn't you see the gun right under his hand?"

I turned and looked at her. I said, "I don't have a gun right now." I went through the narrow doorway and found myself in a tiny private washroom with a clothes closet, a mirror and all the trimmings.

I ran the cold water faucet and carefully washed the blood out of my hair. As well as I could see the scalp wound was not deep. It had been enough to knock me cold and as always that part of the head bled profusely. I guess it was that that had saved my life—if Lardner had known I was still breathing, he'd have pumped another slug into me for sure.

I had my collar loosened off, and I wiped down my shirt and tuxedo and found a comb and fixed myself so I looked at least reasonably human. Then I went back inside.

There were two more people there. A guy and a woman, and from the way they stared at me I knew they were more members of the household staff.

Hubbard said, "I advise you—not to give trouble—young man!"

I saw someone had fed him a cannon. It was a big, old army .45 and he was holding it in both hands. It weaved around a little and I didn't like the look of that big gun in his shaking hands.

I said, "Okay, take it easy. I'll stick around until the cops come."

I went and sat in the armchair. They all stood and watched me. Then Genevieve Troy said with obvious effort, "We—we thought you were dead, lying there."

"I guess I did, too. It was only a scalp wound. Too bad about that." I added, "A condemned guy gets privileges, huh?"

There was silence, all staring at me like I was an exhibit in some freak show.

I snapped my fingers, "Cigarette, buster!"

The guy standing close to Hubbard jerked forward. He was dressed in shirt and pants and had the lean, knowing look of a chauffeur. He fumbled in his pants' pocket and took out a pack of cigarettes and a lighter, which he held out to me gingerly, as if he were afraid I might explode right in his face.

I took the cigarettes and the lighter. I made a light and pushed the rest of the pack in my pocket.

He backed away from me sharply.

I said, "Look, Hubbard, point that gun someplace else, huh?"

Genevieve Troy seemed to have recovered her nerve. She said, "All of you get out of here. Except you, Hubbard. You keep guard over him. The police will be here presently." She looked me right in the eye. "It's quite obvious what happened. This man broke in here. My husband discovered him. He took his gun out of the drawer there and fired at this man—and was promptly killed."

There was silence. The other two staff members had moved to the door but lingering, like they didn't want to miss anything.

Hubbard said without taking his eyes off me—or his gun either, "Mrs. Troy, do you know this man?"

"I believe he's Larry Kent, a New York detective. I saw his picture in a Los Angeles paper only a day or two ago."

She lied real smooth.

Hubbard said, "A detective? But what on earth would he want—?"

"I don't know what he wanted," snapped Genevieve. "It's up to the police to find out the truth of this. I'm going to call Walt Coburn on the hall phone."

She went out. I saw that somebody had thrown a sheet over the old guy by the desk. I dragged at my cigarette in silence for a moment, then I said, "Where did the old guy get it, Hubbard?"

"In the head." His pudgy lips were working. "As if you didn't know."

There was another silence.

Hubbard broke it, "I guess you killed the old man for what you could get."

"Maybe."

"Being a detective you'd know that he kept all that money in the private wall-safe."

"Sure," I said. "Why else would I want to bump him off?"

Hubbard said, "You're callous, but you won't get that money now and you won't be so brash when they put you in the chair."

I got up, looked around for some place to stub my cigarette and found none, dropped it on the flags between two scatter rugs, and trod on it.

I said, "You're way off beam. That safe's empty."

He exclaimed, "How do you—" then broke off.

Genevieve was back with a rush. "Hubbard, they're here."

He turned round to face her. "The police, ma'am?"

"Yes. Three car loads. They just drove up. You'd better go and let them in."

"But I can't leave him, ma'am!"

"I'll watch him." She took the gun from his hands. He seemed reluctant to part with it. "Don't worry, Hubbard, he won't get away from me."

"As you say, ma'am."

From way off I could hear the insistent pealing of a doorbell.

Hubbard hurried out without giving me a further glance.

Genevieve waited only a few seconds, then hurried over to me, her house gown rustling against her long legs.

"Larry," she said urgently. "What's your price?"

I said, "I'm fresh out."

"If you play along, I'll give you—" She hesitated, and then, "Fifty thousand dollars."

"That's a lot of chips."

"It's my price. I haven't time to haggle What's it to be, Larry?"

I said, "If the cops find me here I'm a dead duck."

"They won't."

I stared at her.

She gestured with her gun toward the door set in an alcove beyond the desk. "That's the way Lardner got in and out again. The lock's been broken—"

"To make it look like I got in the hard way?"

"Larry—they're coming!" She pushed against me. Her eyes were big, staring. "I didn't kill my husband, but now I'm in so deep I can't get out. Play along with me and—"

I could hear voices booming through the house.

"Okay," I said. "I'll go this far."

"Hit me," she said. "And make it look good."

"It'll be a pleasure," I told her.

I took the gun from her fingers. I slugged her on the side of the head. As she toppled to her knees I said, "I guess that'll show."

I jumped across the room, through the alcove, plucked open the door that swung with shattered lock. I plunged out into the darkness. For a moment I hesitated then ran down a short walk, cut through tall shrubs and headed for open country.

I had taken only a dozen paces when a patrol car nosed slowly round the side of the house, its red roof light blinking on and off.

I heard a voice say, "You guys better spill around back there—"

I didn't wait to hear any more. I dived back toward the shrubbery. Some keen-eyed cop must have seen the move. I heard a sharp exclamation and then, "The light, quick!"

I was a couple of paces from the shrubbery when a heavy light hit the ground a yard away, swept over me, came back and held me, pinned like a moth.

"Get him!"

A shot screamed over my head.

I whirled about, my hands up. One thing I didn't want right then was to wind up with a police bullet in my guts.

They were pouring toward me. I could see the gleam of a sub-machine gun.

They swarmed about me and took the .45 I'd snatched from Genevieve.

"Better take him into the house."

They hustled me toward glass doors that stood already open. The whole of that great house was blazing with lights.

The guys in blue had me right in there, holding me like they meant business and then a fresh voice cut through, "All right, boys."

I found I was facing a tall, long-faced guy with hard eyes, a plain-clothes guy who said abruptly, "I'm Lieutenant Mark Isles, Los Angeles Homicide Bureau. I'm arresting you for the murder of Jacob Troy. All right, boys, take him in."

The cell didn't have mod cons in it, it didn't even have radio. The jailer held the door wide for me and as I stepped out I said, "Those magazine stories are cockeyed."

He stared at me.

I said, "No radios, no television, no home comforts. I expected more from Los Angeles."

"Keep walkin', bud."

I walked down the echoing corridor and round a sharp bend into a room that had a grille door set flush in one wall.

"Far enough. Stand right there. Put out your hands."

I put them out. They'd already printed me. I felt something cold against my wrists, and for the first time in a long time heard the snap of manacles. I glanced at my wrists, then I looked up.

Mark Isles was standing with arms folded watching me. Back of him were four or five plainclothes cops and there were uniformed guys all around the room.

"Okay," I said. "Make it stick."

The expression on Isles' face didn't change, but a plump cop beside him said, "It's Kent, all right. I knew him way back, before I came West."

I looked at the fat guy but his face didn't mean a thing.

Isles said, "Bring him over here."

They led me over to a hard chair, sited directly beneath an arching lamp with a metal shade. The room lights went out. Somebody snapped a switch and as I sat down, the full amperage of the lamp hit me in the face.

Mark Isles was standing just beyond the pool of light and I was aware of other cops ringed around.

Isles' voice came cold, measured, "You care to tell us about this thing?"

"Sure," I said, "I'll tell you just about everything you want, Isles, only I don't like being made a pigeon."

As if I hadn't spoken he said, "I'll set up the facts for you just so you'll remember better. You were arrested attempting to escape from the house in which Jacob Troy had been killed. He was shot once through the head with a .32 caliber Belgian pistol whose registration number corresponds with that on the police identity card found in your wallet. That .32, according to the testimony of certain people in the house, was found lying at your side when the discovery of the body was first made. It has fingerprints on it, and experts have established that they belong to you."

His voice seemed to be coming from a long way off—and the recountal of facts was as gloomy as the sound of nails being hammered into my coffin. I started to feel not so good.

"Under the dead man's hand was found a .40-.40 pistol which was registered in Jacob Troy's name and which he habitually kept in the top drawer of his desk in the library. The gun had been fired and the bullet was found embedded in the wall. We assume that it was that bullet that caused the scalp wound in your head."

I didn't deny it. I didn't say anything. There was no point in saying anything.

Isles went on, "It's fairly easy for us to reconstruct just what happened back there at Burnt Springs, but what we want now is the motive, just why you did it, Kent? What was back of your visit to Burnt Springs? Why did you break in by way of that side door and what were you after? We take it maybe you didn't mean to kill the old guy, but he came at you with a gun, let fly at you and you fired back before you blacked out. That's straightforward. Now you give us the dope on why you did it, huh?"

I said, "I'll make a statement."

"You tell it."

"I'll write a statement and sign it."

"You dictate it."

"Okay," I said. "Take these fancy bracelets off, give me a cigarette and a drink and I'll tell you what you want to know."

There was a long silence and then Isles said, "You're not in New York now, Kent."

"You figure I'd demand special treatment in New York?"

"Maybe you would."

"For the record, I don't often sit around in the Tombs being quizzed by cops for a killing I didn't do."

Somebody laughed and the fat guy who reckoned he knew me said out of the darkness, "Why don't these guys get a new line? Always they say they never done it."

Isles said, "Kent, you better come across. Before you get out of that chair you're going to admit you killed Jacob Troy."

I said nothing.

"Just let's hear you say it, Kent. Make with the words, man. You'll make it easier for yourself."

"Go to hell."

An arm moved across my line of vision. I saw something dangling from the hand at the end of the arm.

So it was going to be a rubber hose after all.

Isles said, "Hold it, Mac." And then, "I'll give you one last chance, Kent. Did you kill Jacob Troy?"

"No," I said, "I didn't. And I changed my mind about making that statement. You'll get nothing out of me. Now get your hose working."

Again there was silence and somebody whispered something but it didn't carry to me.

Isles said sharply, "Knock off the light."

The light was snapped off. The room light sprang up. A guy came through the door at the far side of the room. He was a slim, almost shabby guy, but there was something about his face that made me look twice at him. He stopped in the middle of the room, glanced incuriously at me and then turned to Isles and said, "How you making out?"

The cop replied awkwardly, "Not so good, Belasco."

Belasco said, "You're way out of date on your methods, lieutenant."

I saw a flush spring to Isles' face. He growled something and Belasco replied calmly, "You'll get no place this way. Take those things off him and have him brought round to my office." He turned on his heel and went out of the room.

All the cops stared at me. I could see the hate on their faces. I got up out of the chair, held out my wrists.

"Okay," growled Isles. "Take them off."

A cop put his key in my handcuffs and snapped them off.

I shook my wrists. "What kind of weight does Belasco haul around here?"

Isles said, "He only happens to be the District Attorney. But don't run away with any ideas he's going to use you light. When he leans on you, brother, you'll think the City Hall fell on you. All right, Mac. Four of you take him down to the car." He added, "If he makes a break, shoot him."

4

Mister Big

Vincent Callendar was quick. I heard afterward that he had waited about an hour for me at the Santa Rosa then gone back inside and discovered I'd already left. Figuring I'd taken a cab back to town, he drove home then called my hotel without success. He went back into Los Angeles and there ran into a crime writer from the Chronicle, who gave him the buzz about Jacob Troy's murder. He also told Callendar that there was a rumor of a surprise twist to the killing, although the cops hadn't released the name of the guy they were holding as suspect. All the Chronicle man knew was that the suspect was supposed to be an out-of-town detective.

Callendar had at once made a call to a contact in the Police Department to check if it was me—and now here he was, sitting in the D.A.'s office when the four cops body-guarded me in.

"Sit down there," said the D.A. indicating a chair to one side of his desk.

As I sat down he nodded to the cops. "All right, I won't need you."

The cop called Mac hesitated.

"Lieutenant Isles said—"

"I don't care what he said," broke in Belasco sharply. "One of you men wait outside the door. The rest can go back to headquarters."

Looking uneasy, the cops filed out.

Joseph Belasco, who had held office in that district for the past five years, was in his early forties but looked older. I remembered that he had made a name for himself as a junior on Kleiner's staff and that he was regarded as a hot prospect as the next State Governor. Having seen the reaction of the cops to his authority, I figured that he'd have to make more friends before he achieved that high office. Maybe that was his trouble; he was too smart and too forthright for the run-of-the-mill administration.

He perched himself on the corner of his desk, took a half-burned cigar from a tray and proceeded to light it. The silence was oppressive.

He puffed on his cigar, drew it from his mouth and regarded it critically, then without looking at me said in an unemotional tone of voice, "All right, Kent, let's have it."

"Just one moment Mr. District Attorney." Callendar was on his feet. "I've already given you a statement and I would like to present myself on behalf of Larry Kent as his counsel—"

"No you won't," broke in Belasco. He was still studying the glowing end of his cigar. "You can sit in on this as Kent's friend, but if you're going to insist on representing him legally, I'll have to ask you to wait outside."

Callendar protested, "That's hardly ethical, D.A.—"

"I'm not interested in ethics right now," replied Belasco. He waved the cigar stub in the air, making thin spirals of smoke. "Right now we're sifting a murder. Looks like your friend, Kent, here, is in quite a spot. I'm not satisfied that he killed Jacob Troy and that's why we've got him over here, but I might as well point out right away, Callendar, I can hold him only for so long. Once I throw him back to the Police Department your guess is as good as mine what'll happen to him."

Callendar gave an angry laugh. "That sure is laying it on the line. If you're going to issue an indictment for homicide against Kent, I insist on representing him and looking over any statement which he is asked to sign. I don't want to sound difficult, D.A., but—"

"You are," said Belasco flatly. He dropped the stub in the tray without smoking it further. He swung round on Callendar, folding his arms across his skimpy chest. "This is the position. Kent's on the spot. I want to hear just why he got that way. Maybe you can help out. When we're through, I'll form my own opinions and we'll see where we go from there. Is that clear, or do I have to put a little weight behind my words?"

Callendar swallowed, then muttered, "You can't blame me for feeling this way. I got a considerable shock tonight when I heard the news."

"You weren't the only one," said Belasco impassively. "All right, Callendar, suppose you sit down and relax, huh?"

Without a word Vincent Callendar sat back in his chair. He looked plenty unhappy.

I said, "I'll clear the air, Belasco."

He looked at me. "Well?"

"I didn't kill Jacob Troy. Next question."

He went on staring at me. I saw his eyes were a peculiarly penetrating gray-blue. There was intelligence back of those eyes—but I reminded myself that that intelligence could be dangerous if Belasco started leaning on me the way Isles had promised he would.

The silence lasted a couple of minutes, then, still staring at me, he said, "Callendar, you give it to me. What are the circumstances of Kent being over here?"

"I told you," replied Callendar resentfully. "I hired him to come out here to make some investigations for me."

"Such as what investigations?"

"I don't think I'm at liberty right now—"

Belasco slid off the desk so fast Callendar blinked. "Look, mister, don't horse around. This is a homicide rap. Which way you want it to go? Against Kent?"

Silence.

"All right, who's he investigating? And why?"

"A client of mine," muttered Callendar.

"Troy?"

"Oh, no." Callendar gave a short laugh. "Walt Coburn still handles Troy's legal affairs to my knowledge. He should have been struck off the lawyers' list years ago, but that's the way it goes."

"Okay, who is your client?"

"Paul Huntsman."

"Out at the Santa Rosa?"

"That's right."

Belasco climbed back on the table, perched there, swinging his skinny legs, his hands clamping the desk either side of him.

"Go on, Callendar."

Vincent said, "Huntsman's been bothered plenty by concessionaires. The rackets have moved in on him."

"Did he make any complaints to the law?"

"No," said Callendar. He moved his feet awkwardly and stared at his hands. "It hadn't got that far."

"Yet you had to call in a private eye. Right?"

"I guess you could say that."

"I am saying it. And now I'm asking you what you wanted Kent to do for you with regard to Huntsman in these vague rackets you talk about."

Callendar said heavily. "There were no specific duties. Huntsman had the feeling that the squeeze was on him." Callendar got up and moved slowly over to the desk. Standing close to Belasco he said, "This is really it, D.A. Huntsman was being squeezed by Jacob Troy."

Leaning back in my chair I was watching Belasco's face. It didn't change expression.

He said, "And did you want Kent to work on Troy?"

Callendar swallowed. He said, "I can see you're way ahead of me. You're figuring that Kent went and shook Troy down a little and Troy got mean and pulled a gun and—"

Belasco raised a hand. "It's you who's way ahead of yourself, brother. Suppose you tell it in your own words, huh? And leave me to figure out my own conclusions."

From my chair, I said, "Why fool around, Callendar? You're not doing anybody any good, myself most of all."

Vincent Callendar said aggrievedly, "I'm only trying to do my best!"

"Then do better." I got to my feet. "I'll save time. Huntsman got the idea Troy was working on him through Danny Hester."

"Ah," said Belasco. "Now we get down to names." He added shrewdly, "Knowing your record, Kent, I guess it isn't often you put the finger on a guy, even a racketeer like Hester. Right?"

"You know about him?"

Belasco nodded. "In my job I get to know plenty things before they hit the broadsheets. Hester's been operating a long time undercover. I guess it's only lately he's been coming out and showing his strength. All right, Kent, so you've put the finger squarely on this guy, what you got to back it up with?"

Callendar started to say something but I rode over him, "Huntsman's idea was that Hester was the link. I was to try and get close to him through one of his hatchet men whom I knew back East, years ago."

"His name?"

I shrugged. It had to come out sooner or later, so why not now? "Al Lardner."

"No-Face," said Belasco instantly. I saw a gleam in his eyes.

"Yeah," I said. "Quite a character. You got anything on him?"

"We have," he replied. "I guess we can pick him up anytime, but right now he doesn't matter. Let's have it, Kent."

I said, "Huntsman was wrong about Hester operating from Troy's headquarters. It's my hunch he was working independently—out to get Huntsman's territory, including the gambling layout at the Santa Rosa. Get it right, Belasco. Huntsman is operating legitimately."

"You don't have to cover up for him," said Belasco placidly. "I know all about Huntsman. He's an all-right guy. Maybe he bit off more than he could chew when he took on the Santa Rosa and left the door open for the racketeers to move in. Maybe he wasn't so smart at that. Danny Hester, on the other hand, could be too smart." He added, "What makes you think Hester is operating independently of Troy?"

Before I could answer, he went on, "That is assuming that Troy had any interest in Huntsman's affairs?"

Callendar laughed. "Believe you me, Troy was so interested in Huntsman's real estate deals he was really trying."

"To break him?"

"You can put it any way you like. That's what it adds up to."

"Well," said Belasco. It was more a statement than a question. He was looking at me.

I shrugged. "I was interested only in Danny Hester and his activities concerning Huntsman. That's why I was being retained, to get close to the racketeers. Well, tonight I got too close."

"Meaning?"

"Huntsman had a twister in the camp—one of his close guys double-crossed him and I was set for the long drop. Hester's boys shook me down out there at the Santa Rosa and pushed me around a little. Maybe the scars still show."

"Yeah," said Belasco, "I was wondering about the marks."

Callendar exclaimed, "Larry, just what happened?"

"Another time," I told him. "You want it on the line, Belasco, here it is. I was framed for that killing. Danny Hester had me on the spot and left me there with a pile of evidence a mile high. The idea was to kill me right there on the spot, but I guess I was lucky."

There was silence for a moment and then Belasco said quietly, "You'll have to make this stick, Kent."

"Sure."

"Was Lardner in it?"

"He was the triggerman."

"Got any idea why Hester would want to rub old Troy out?"

"Maybe he's got ideas of taking over his territory, too."

He snapped, "Troy was not a racketeer, whatever else."

I shrugged. "You can call him what you like, it makes no difference. I guess he was the closest we'll ever get to having a robber baron in the U.S. He started off legitimately and the more power he got the more he wanted—newspaper owner—backer of movie productions—realty king—he made his twenty million and wouldn't call it quits. The methods he used to get that high could qualify him for the title of racketeer. However, we won't argue over it."

"I'm not arguing with anybody," replied Belasco pleasantly. "It seems to me you have the score very thoroughly, Kent, but—" He crossed his arms and nursed his elbows. "Maybe you can give me proof that Hester rubbed old Troy out, using Lardner as the triggerman. Maybe you can prove that you were put on the spot—guys will go to great lengths to prove their innocence when they're just one jump off the electric chair. You with me, Kent?"

"Sure," I said.

"Okay. Make it stick."

***

At the time I was being grilled in the detectives' room at police headquarters and having my session with the District Attorney—at the same time the City Coroner's assistants were working on the body of Jacob Troy as it lay on the slab at the police morgue—a conference was being held in the home of Mrs. Mildred Delamore.

As Vince Callendar had told me earlier, Mrs. Mildred Delamore was Jacob Troy's widowed sister—her old man had taken a long jump off the cliff at Lucinda Beach after being put through the mincing machine by Jacob Troy.

Which maybe made Mildred a little bitter toward her brother. At all events it had produced in her an even stronger desire to protect the interests of her alcoholic son, Rod (the lush I'd tangled with in the bar where I'd met his girlfriend, the Mouse), and for her beauteous daughter, Angel.

Mildred got the news of Jacob Troy's killing from that same crime reporter on the *Chronicle* who had put Vince Callendar wise. This reporter, hot on a story, called up Mildred at her home at Bel-Air and later went out there and interviewed her for his paper. After he left she wasted no time in putting through a call to the Beverly Hills apartment which Angel shared with her brother, Rod. It was a kind of screwy arrangement but I guess that's how the whole family was—nuts.

Angel had been having an early night—maybe she wanted to catch up on her beauty sleep—whatever it was she was right there on tap and she dressed and took a cab round to her mother's house, after calling at several night spots to try and track down her brother, Rod. By chance, one of these messages reached the drink-soused guy at the Palomino, where he was still insisting to the Mouse that this was definitely his last drink. When he got the message, Rod, by all accounts, sobered a little—enough to pass on the news of his uncle's sudden death to the Mouse, who promptly called a cab and bundled him into it and got him round to the mother's place.

In the meantime, Mildred had been busy making further calls, and her brother Willard was already on his way. Willard, as I discovered later, was a big, drooping guy with a permanent stoop both in his shoulders and in his mind. He was one of those guys who never quite make it; success had always just been out of reach. What is more, he had never been able to prise even a half buck out of his celebrated millionaire brother.

So this conference was held whilst I was downtown in Los Angeles trying to lever myself off the hot squat.

You ever seen a bunch of buzzards gathered around a corpse of a once useful but now dead mule?

To find anyone looking less like a vulture than Angel Delamore would be hard to imagine. She was one of those dames who look as luscious as a ripe pear at the age of about fourteen and from there on out they either become world-famous beauties, pin-ups, film stars, models—or they marry some fabulously rich guy at the age of twenty and proceed to settle down for a year or so, and then have the first profitable divorce of a string of five.

Her mother looked more the part: tall, craggy-faced, with a beaked nose, skimpy hair, drawn back in an old fashioned chignon. The only concession to beauty that she made was to wear a couple of rocks on her left hand, a legacy from her dead husband—A. K. Delamore had salted away some of his hard won cash in a few diamonds at a time of temporary prosperity. Mildred Delamore had a habit of waving the rock-laden hand around any time she wanted to impress anybody, which was mostly always.

She figured she was head of the family, so she took the chair at the top of the dining table, which was part of the imported suite she had hung on to through bad times and good. On one side of her sat Rod, already dozing in his chair, and on the other side sat Angel, primly upright on hers, looking as fresh as a daisy and in no need of beauty sleep whatever.

The other end of the table sat brother Willard, stooped, mumbling, not at all happy, because he had a hatred of publicity, and next to him as a concession grudgingly made by Mrs. Delamore, sat Dodo King, the Mouse.

You can imagine for yourself how that conference went. First of all the bald announcement from the head of the table that Jacob Troy had been murdered, nothing surer. Next, the veiled insinuation that cops were falling all over their feet getting no place as to who had killed poor Uncle Jacob. After that came the sixty-four thousand dollar question—who was going to get the dough?

A lot of talk followed the tossing in of that choice morsel. Even Rod woke up and took a share. Through it all the only silent one was the Mouse, who, whilst keenly alive to the prospects of marrying Rod and having a million dollars poured into her lap, was really more interested in watching the reactions of the Delamore family, whom she considered privately to be just a bunch of nuts.

No matter how they talked, no matter where they got, it all wound up to the same thing.

How about Genevieve?

It was around three in the morning when Mildred Delamore made a decision. She got to her feet. The rest of them fell silent. Looking at the Mouse, she said clearly, "My dear, I don't like to bother my maid this time of night. Would you be so kind as to make us some coffee?"

"Of course, Mrs. Delamore." The Mouse got to her feet, bright and eager, her orange-colored hair flaming in the soft light of the antique fitting above her head. She was the kind of dame who never worried over sleep. She could keep on going all day and all night if need be—just so somebody fed her a hooker of gin occasionally or stimulated her with a little lively conversation.

"You'll find everything in the kitchen, my dear," purred Mildred smoothly. "I'm sure you can make out just fine."

"Leave it to me," said the Mouse brightly, and smiled at Rod who stared back at her blearily, and left the room.

The minute the door closed behind her Mildred sat down in her chair, hard. Leaning over the table she said, "I think we're all decided on one thing."

They looked at her expectantly.

"Genevieve must not get Jacob's money."

***

Belasco reached across the desk and flicked down the switch of the talk-back. "Get me Lieutenant Isles at headquarters." He snapped back the switch, went round the desk and sat in his chair. Linking his fingers together he looked at me and said, "I'm going to send out an alarm on Danny Hester and on Al Lardner. What did you say the name of the other guy was?"

"I didn't say."

"Let's have it, Kent."

I shrugged. "Nick Pullen."

"That the guy who was at the Santa Rosa?" Callendar exclaimed, "Larry, don't tell me Pullen double-crossed Huntsman?"

"Yeah, he's on Hester's payroll. What else you got in mind, Belasco?"

The D.A. stared at me in silence for a moment and then, "I'm still waiting for that proof, Kent."

"I told you I couldn't make anything stick unless I was mobile."

"That's all very well, as far as it goes. Sure I can free you, but—" The phone on his desk started ringing. He reached out, picked up the receiver. "Yes, Isles. I want you to send out a call on Danny Hester. Know him?" He gave a short laugh. "Yeah, I bet you do. Any idea where you can pick him up fast? I want him. I want his henchmen, too, Al Lardner, Nick Pullen." Isles must have started squawking down the wire about me, because Belasco said, "I've got a new line on Kent. I shan't hold him for further questioning. Not right away. How's that?" He listened and then, "Leave me to be the judge of that, lieutenant. Just get hold of Hester. Have him down here at the City Hall for a talk, huh?" He hung up and looked at me. "They might pick up Hester right away and then again—"

I broke in, "Five gets you ten he won't be brought in tonight."

"It's morning," said Belasco, pleasantly. He glanced at the window. Pale daylight was already showing. "Where are you staying in town, Kent?"

"The Sheridan Hotel."

"You'll be on call there if we need you."

"Sure."

"Once Hester's brought in we'll most likely have you down here right away." He turned to Vince Callendar. "I would suggest you advise your client, Paul Huntsman, to put his house in order. If he's got any specific charges of racketeering against Hester, he can file them with my office."

Callendar nodded mutely.

"Apart from that," went on Belasco crisply, "Huntsman better mend the roof on that house of his, else he could be answering awkward questions in this office, too."

"Okay," said Callendar quietly, "I get it."

Belasco moved round our side of the desk. He looked at me and said, "You're free to go."

"Thanks."

"There's one thing you maybe should know before you do go. I took the testimony of the people at Troy's house before I got back here. That testimony is conflicting. According to Mrs. Genevieve Troy, she saw somebody running away in the darkness, a few moments after she found the body of her husband, with you lying a few feet away, shot, as she thought, dead." A grim smile came on to his mouth. "Mrs. Troy would hardly be lying about a thing like that, now would she, Kent?"

I said nothing.

Belasco nodded. As if satisfied he said, "Mrs. Genevieve Troy is a fine woman. What would you say?"

"I hadn't noticed."

He took a step toward me. "Kent, put it on the line. What happened after Hubbard left you alone with her? That is, just when the police were arriving?"

I said, "She was waving a gun around. I was nervous it might go off. I took it from her. She started clawing at me so I slugged her."

"Just like that, huh?"

"Yeah."

"You slugged her but not real hard."

I shrugged.

"She just had one of these itzy-bitzy bruises on the side of her face. You usually slug dames that easy?"

"I wouldn't know."

"I would," said Belasco. "Okay, so Mrs. Troy saw somebody running away from the scene of the crime, like the books say. Kind of lets you out."

"I was let out all the time, Belasco."

"Not by my book. You're guilty as hell until you prove it otherwise."

Callendar burst out, "Why didn't you tell us you had this testimony of Genevieve Troy's before you started grilling Kent?"

Belasco didn't look at him. He said, "Sometime I'll come round to your law office, Callendar, and tell you how to run your business, huh?"

There was silence.

Belasco moved to the door, opened it. He said to the cop on duty, "Okay, get back to headquarters." He jerked his head at me. "You're walking out, Kent, but pull a smooth one on me and I'll have you back here so fast you won't know what hit you. Got it?"

"Sure," I said. "You taking me up on that bet about arresting Danny Hester?"

He said, "Maybe I'll put a patrolman on to tail you around, Kent. Maybe you could lead us to Hester. What do you say?"

I said nothing.

Callendar went out.

I followed him.

The door closed. We went along to the elevator. The big cop was standing there, waiting for the elevator to come up. He glared at us, said nothing. We rode down in the elevator in complete silence.

Out on the street the daylight was breaking cold. There was a slight drizzle in the air and no hint of sun coming out of the gray clouds banked in the east.

I said to Callendar, "Sunny California, huh?"

He said impatiently, "Look at that cop go. Bet you he heads back to headquarters and has Isles stick a couple of shadows on you."

"Why not?" I shrugged and walked down the street and he padded along after.

There was a drugstore already open. I went in there, bought cigarettes, and as I broke the seal I said, "I'm going back to my hotel. I'll see you at ten o'clock in the Pacific Grill."

"Now, wait a bit—"

"I'm going to get some sleep." I went out, flagged down a crawling taxi and headed for the Hotel Sheridan.

5

Don't go near the water ...

The early-duty clerk eyed me thoughtfully.

"You want to change your room, Mr. Kent?"

"That's what I said."

"Well, I guess it can be arranged, but—" He hesitated.

I took out my billfold and slid out a ten spot, crumpled it and dropped it on the counter in front of him.

His eyes flicked down to it then back to me. "I'm sure it can be arranged, Mr. Kent."

"Make the change-over while I'm having myself a drink."

"I'm afraid there's nobody on duty, Mr. Kent—it's a little early—"

"Fix it for me," I told him.

"Very well, Mr. Kent." I saw his hand close over the ten spot. "Have you any particular preference for a room?"

"Any place as long as it's got four walls and a window. And—" I added, "I'm not all that fussy about a window. Just quiet."

He nodded. "I'm sorry that your original room wasn't comfortable—"

"It was okay," I broke in. "I just want a change, that's all. Okay by you?"

"Of course, Mr. Kent."

"Also," I told him. "Anybody comes here asking for me, call me through but not before nine o'clock. I'm going to get myself some sleep."

"Sure, Mr. Kent. If you go through into the small lounge back there

I'll see that you have a drink."

"Double Scotch," I told him. "Make it two."

I went through to the lounge, dropped into a chair and lit a cigarette. So I was changing my room. I was making things just a little harder for Danny Hester, just in case he was still on liberty.

What's more I wasn't taking any chances with Genevieve.

I slept three hours, got up, shaved, ran a shower and called room service for a bottle of whisky.

I glanced out the window and saw it was still drizzling rain. My new room was on the twentieth floor and I had a swell view of the low hanging clouds. To hell with the weather.

I went through to the shower recess, peeled off my pajamas and soaked out the ache from my muscles. Then I ran the cold water and felt the needles bringing a little more life into the old red corpuscles. As I turned the water off I heard knocking on the door. I reached for my robe, walked through to the door and called, "Who is it?"

"Room service, sir."

I opened the door and a guy came in, glanced at me incuriously and set down a tray bearing a bottle of Scotch and a pitcher of ice.

"Just leave it," I told him. "I'll pour it myself."

He looked at me sharply, then grinned. He was a cheerful, freckle-faced youth.

As I slipped him a buck I said, "Anybody down in the lobby asking after me?"

"I wouldn't know, Mr. Kent."

"Guess you haven't seen me around this morning."

He looked at me. "Just like you say, Mr. Kent." He tossed the screwed up bill in his hand and went out the door, whistling under his breath.

I poured myself a drink and swirled the ice around in it, went back to the window and looked out again. There seemed to be no profit in that, either. I had some more of my drink, set the glass down and put my valise on the bed, fumbled through the spare shirts until I found my spare gun and a clip of ammunition. I had just snapped the magazine into the gun when the phone started ringing.

Carrying the gun in my hand I went over and picked up the receiver. It was the desk.

"There's a phone call for you, Mr. Kent, but I thought I'd better check to see if you're available—"

"Smart of you," I told him. "Who's calling?"

"A Mrs. Troy."

I thought for a minute. "Okay," I said. "Have them put the call through."

Genevieve came on the wire right away. "Larry?"

"Yeah," I said. "How's every little thing this morning?"

"Larry, I've just got to talk with you. I've been trying to get you all morning—"

"I've been around."

"Have you fixed it with your hotel so you don't have to take telephone calls?" There was a note of acid in her voice.

I said, "I've got this whole town fixed, baby."

"Look, Larry, remember our deal last night?"

"Could I forget it? Fifty grand doesn't come my way every day of the year."

"I'm trusting you," she said. There was urgency in her voice. "You know I had no hand in my husband's death—"

"Skip it, baby. I heard the story of goldilocks so long back I lost count."

She said angrily, "All right, you don't have to believe me but—I've got to protect my own interests. I let you go last night, I gave you a break. In return for that I expect you to play along."

"So far," I told her, "I've played along so hard I damn near wound up on the hot squat."

She said eagerly, "Did they question you?"

"What do cops usually do with a murder suspect? Figure it for yourself, baby."

She was silent and I added, "What does Danny make of all this?"

"I haven't see him." Her reply was short.

"Gone into smoke, huh?"

"I don't know what you mean."

"I got a buzz that the cops were out looking for him. Maybe I'm wrong but seems like some guy's fingered your boyfriend. Only a matter of time before he's taken back to City Hall. They've got a cute District Attorney down there. One of those tough guys. Won't take bribes, keen as hell. You know?"

In a tight voice said, "Larry, I can't talk now. But I've just got to see you."

"Okay. When?"

"Right away. Could I come to your hotel?"

"No," I said. "That's out."

"Then you suggest some place—and sometime soon."

"I can hardly wait," I told her. "Only I got a lot on my agenda right now."

"You certainly play hard to get."

"It's a must, baby. You know something? I held back from the District Attorney exactly what did happen last night at that bum castle of yours. You know why I did that? I'll tell you. I don't like being pushed around by racketeers like Danny Hester, nor by big dumb blondes like you, so I figure I'd keep certain things to myself just so you and your boyfriend are at liberty a while longer, giving me time just to see what makes both of you tick. You with me, baby?"

"I'm still here." Her voice was higher than usual, shaking a little.

I went on. "You call it the streak of curiosity in me, or you call it any damn thing you like, I'm sticking around."

I reached out for the pack of cigarettes I'd dropped on the table near the phone. As I juggled one to my mouth I heard her say, "They won't get Danny Hester. Not in a long time."

I said nothing.

"And as for me, why it's unthinkable that they'd ever suspect that I had any hand in my husband's death." Her tone changed suddenly. "I can't talk any more. Hubbard's coming—"

I said, "That butler sure gets around."

"Look, Larry, I'm in terrible trouble. There are reporters, photographers everywhere and the police ... Jacob's death is so big—I never dreamt all this would happen—"

She broke off. "Look, Larry, will you meet me at a place out of town? I just thought of it. It's a small roadhouse."

"The Santa Rosa?" I asked her.

She gave an angry laugh. "Of course not. I said a small place. We could meet there, talk quietly."

"About what, baby?"

"You want that fifty thousand, don't you?"

"Do I want to breathe?"

"Very well, then. I'll forget what you said about wanting to get even with Danny and me. I'll just forget all about that and meet you as an equal, Larry."

"That's mighty big of you. Where is this place?"

"It's called the Pelican. It's on the highway about ten miles from Burnt Springs, Los Angeles side. You can't miss it. It's a sort of pink place and it's got a neon sign right on the highway."

"Okay," I said. "What time?"

"Eleven o'clock."

"Make it noon."

"And Larry—"

I said, "See you then, baby."

I hung up.

Thoughtfully I lit my cigarette. I wondered about Genevieve. She had been married to one of the richest guys in the country and by all the laws she stood to inherit a package when he died. He was old, he was feeble, she only had to give him a few more years and he'd have checked out without any hastening from a .32 slug. But instead of waiting for him to die, so she could collect, she had tied in with an up-and-coming racketeer, a gangster who was already building up an empire by using guys like Paul Huntsman to extend his domain.

And Genevieve had been right there when Hester had the old guy killed and tried to frame me for it.

Why?

It just didn't add up. I'd called her a dumb blonde, but she wasn't that, I knew. She was smart enough to know that there was always a risk of being fingered for the murder of her husband, no matter how it was fixed, and I had a hunch that the actual triggering was made on impulse when they had me in their hands, a guy they figured was perfect for a frame-up.

So she was ready to take the risk. She wanted the old guy bumped off.

For what?

If she was due to inherit, all she had to do was wait.

Which could mean that she wasn't going to inherit at all.

I dragged on my cigarette. It tasted bitter. I mashed it out in the tray, picked up the glass and had myself a drink.

Then an idea hit me like I'd been sandbagged from behind.

How about if old man Troy, shrewd as a barrel full of monkeys, had tumbled to Genevieve's two-timing him with Danny Hester? Could be that he'd used Hester. Huntsman's idea could have been right to a point—that Troy had made use of Hester's undercover organization in order to muscle in on Huntsman's real estate deals. And when Jacob Troy got wise to Genevieve maybe he drew up a new will and cut her right out.

I milled this over in my mind. Thinking made me thirsty.

I poured myself another Scotch.

The phone rang.

I took my time picking up the receiver. Looked like I was in for a busy day.

It was the helpful clerk again. "I'm sorry to worry you, Mr. Kent, but there's another call for you—you still want all callers checked?"

"You're making out fine," I told him. "Who is it this time?"

"Mr. Walt Coburn."

I thought fast. "The attorney?"

"I believe so, sir. He says he's representing the estate of the late Jacob Troy."

"Put him through."

A thin excited nasal voice came down the wire. "That Larry Kent?"

"Yeah."

"This is Walt Coburn. Hiya."

I said nothing but reached out again for the pack of cigarettes.

Coburn said cheerfully, "All kinds of rumors buzzing around town this morning, Mr. Kent. I figure you and me might have a talk about them."

"Why?"

He laughed. It sounded as phony as hell. "The way I heard it, you were right in the thick of things out at Burnt Springs last night. The cops pulled you in for questioning, I believe?"

"You believe plenty," I told him. "What's with you, Coburn? Looking for cheap inside information or what?"

"Now don't get sore at me, mister. I was Jacob Troy's attorney for twenty-five years. I knew all about the old guy, may he rest in peace." He paused and added deliberately, "I don't represent Mrs. Genevieve Troy."

"Too bad. Looks like you're fresh out of a job."

"Oh, no," he laughed. "Far from it, Mr. Kent. I've got plenty things to wind up before I draw up my final account on the Troy estate. You see—there are other interested parties in the Troy family and, well—to cut it short, Mr. Kent—"

"Thanks," I told him.

"I figured we might have a little talk about—shall we say, Mrs. Genevieve Troy's part in the affair last night?"

I said nothing and the wire sang between us. I stared at the blank wall in front of me and then I said, "Just who are you representing? Jacob Troy's estate or his family."

"Well, in a case like this, Mr. Kent, one has to cast his lines in many waters."

"Uh-huh."

"For instance, Mrs. Mildred Delamore now. She's most interested in certain things relating to the late Mr. Troy's estate. For instance the whereabouts of his private cash box containing something like one million dollars in negotiable bonds."

Bells were ringing in my head. Alarm bells. I said evenly, "You're talking way above my head, Coburn."

"I guessed I might be." He laughed. "That's why I figured we might have a talk. You see, I'm not keen on publicity and at this stage I wouldn't want to cross swords with our respected District Attorney. But the truth is, maybe you can throw a little light on the whereabouts of that cash box—or alternatively just where Mrs. Genevieve Troy figures it might be."

"What makes you think I can throw light on any damn thing, Coburn?"

"Just a hunch, Mr. Kent. Just a hunch."

"You've got rocks in your head," I told him. "Now you tell me what's to stop me calling District Attorney Belasco right away and putting him wise that you're running around making speeches?"

He laughed again, only this time he sounded more confident. "You wouldn't do that, Mr. Kent. You wouldn't go to the District Attorney."

I said nothing.

He went on. "Do we meet? Do we have this little talk?"

"What's on your mind?"

"I have an office downtown. Come along any time. Call me first and I'll be there. I'm listed."

I dropped the receiver on the rest. Now I had plenty to think about. One million dollars negotiable.

That called for a drink.

The phone rang again.

The clerk sounded almost apologetic. "You're very popular this morning, Mr. Kent."

"Yeah," I said. "Have them take their place in the line."

"It's a lady this time, calling on you personally."

I figured Genevieve hadn't wasted any time. I said, "Did she drop a name at the counter?"

"Why yes, Mr. Kent. It's Miss Dodo King." He said it like he had a bad taste in his mouth.

I said, "Have her come up."

She was looking as cute and fresh as a cosmetic ad in a glossy magazine.

"I'm so sorry," she said. "Did I get you out of bed?"

"I've been like this for days."

She laughed. She was wearing a green slicker over a dull brown dress that looked like wool but was probably synthetic. But there was nothing phony about the way that dress was molded to her figure; not even the shapeless slicker could cancel out those lines.

"I suppose you wonder why I'm here?"

"I quit wondering about anything when I started shaving."

She laughed again. "Mind if I shed this? I'm a little wet."

"Go right ahead," I said. "Be my guest."

She peeled off her slicker.

I took it from her and threw it on the chair. "Have yourself a drink," I told her. "I'll be right out."

I went through to the bathroom and started to dress. I left the door open. I heard her singing to herself.

I called out, "You always get this way on a wet day in Los Angeles?"

"Most always," she said. "Larry, I don't like Scotch."

"Tough." I tightened the belt about my waist. I was starting to feel more human—especially with that orange headed dame out there. I went out fixing my tie.

She was standing over by the window, a glass in her hand. "Just to be neighborly," she told me, "I guess I can swallow this."

I picked up the harness of my shoulder-holster and strapped it on. I felt her eyes were on me.

"Looks like you're expecting trouble."

"I always expect it."

"Maybe you're right at that. Especially now," she added with meaning.

I got my jacket and shrugged into it, smoothing it down over the bulge under my armpit. I loaded my pocket with keys, wallet, billfold.

"I'll have a cigarette, too." She had her hand outstretched.

I gave her one and made a light.

She moved over to the bed and sat on the edge of it, crossed her ankles demurely. She looked smaller than she had the night before. Cute enough to eat.

I said, "I'll ring through for some gin if it'll make you any happier."

"I'm okay. I'm doing fine. Larry, why don't you sit down?"

"I can take it better on my feet."

She laughed. "Take what? My being here?"

I shrugged. The smoke was wreathing between us.

"All right," she said, "I'll tell you why I came. It was sheer impulse. I know I'm crazy and you'll probably throw me out but—"

"You don't have to apologize," I broke in. "Always glad to meet citizens of this fine town."

She sipped at her drink and made a wry face. "You were in a lot of trouble last night, weren't you, Larry?"

"That what you came up to tell me about?"

"Now quit being difficult. I'm on your side really."

"I didn't even know I had a side."

"I hope it's the best one." She paused. She bit at her lower lip thoughtfully. "Guess none of us had much sleep last night," she said as if at random.

"Uh-huh?"

"Specially the Delamore family."

I pulled a chair toward me and hooked one foot on the seat and leaned on my knee. "Delamore family, huh?"

"You've heard of them?"

"Maybe."

"They're quite a bunch of screwballs." She added, "Especially Rod."

I guess my eyebrows went up. "The boyfriend?"

"He was." She slid off the bed and moved over to the table and banged her glass down. She turned on me as if with decision. "Larry, I broke with Rod this morning. Don't ask me what time. I've lost all count of hours but—his Uncle Jacob dying made all the difference."

"To what?"

"To—well I guess our relationship. You know, I'd quite made up my mind to marry that alcoholic guy, but now—"

She shrugged. "I guess he's aiming higher now he's got the scent of all the millions Jacob's supposed to have left."

"Does Rod figure some of the lucre will go his way?"

"Possibly. At all events he feels differently about me this morning—it all began early this morning. As a matter of fact I want to tell you about it."

"Just why, baby?"

She came right over to me, grabbed my foot and pushed it off the chair. Then she sat on the chair, looked up at me, her feet barely touching the floor.

"Last night—rather, early this morning, Rod got the news of his uncle's death. He was with me of course, and I went right along with him to his mother's house in Bel-Air. It was what they called a family gathering."

"And you went along?"

"Oh, sure," she said indifferently. "I guess Mildred Delamore has gotten around to accepting me. As a matter of fact I think she figured I was good for Rod—how she loves that boy!" She gave a short laugh. "If she hadn't spoiled him quite so much when he was younger, maybe he wouldn't be such a pampered lush today."

I went over to the wall and leaned against it and lighted a fresh cigarette. I let her talk.

"At all events I went along with Rod and even sat in on this family gathering I told you about. Mildred was there, of course and Angel. That's Rod's sister."

"Yeah," I said, "I heard about her."

"Haven't you met her yet? Larry, you haven't lived."

"Keep talking," I said. "Anything's better than watching rain in Los Angeles."

She made a little face at me. She said, "Of course Uncle Willard was there in all his glory. About as cheerful as an undertaker—and underneath just bubbling with joy at the thought that his brother Jacob was dead and that there was bound to be trouble for the family before the estate was wound up."

"Hold it right there," I said. "Old Troy's brother, his sister, her kids. What hopes do they have to carving up Troy's estate?"

"I guess they don't have much," she said with a little laugh. "By all accounts Jacob hated them. He never could get along with his sister and he despised his brother. As for Rod, he wouldn't let him near the place and the only one he had any time for was Angel. In fact he helped her quite a lot when she was trying to break into movies." She shrugged. "I guess the family's pinning a lot of hope on that. But—whatever else, they're determined to upset Jacob's will and state their claims when the time comes."

"What's all this leading up to, baby?"

The Mouse said, "Well, having got a lot off their chests about Uncle Jacob and what trouble there'd be, and how the family stood, and so forth, they got me out of the room—Mildred was so tactful; she got me to make coffee for them. When I was coming back with the coffee I heard your name mentioned and—well, frankly, Larry, I listened at the door."

"Bully for you," I told her. "Get earache?"

"I wasn't exactly at the keyhole," she snapped, "but I did hear what they were saying. It was plenty. After a time I forgot all about the coffee and let it go cold on the tray. I just leaned against the wall there and gathered it all in." She jumped off the chair and moved over to me. "Larry, somebody phoned Mrs. Delamore while I was out in the kitchen. I heard the bell and the mumbled talk. From what I heard in the doorway it seemed it was an attorney called Walt Coburn."

"Uh-huh?"

"He must have put them wise to the fact that you were mixed up in the murder of Jacob Troy. I heard the family say that you were right in it up to your chin, probably in cahoots with Genevieve. How they hate her! Boy, talk about character assassination! I bet Genevieve's ears were burning red."

"Move along baby, you're getting no place fast."

"All right." She sighed and leaned against me as if it was the most natural thing in the world. "I gathered from that talk Jacob Troy was in the habit of keeping a lot of money in his house—he was a crackpot, and in spite of all his holding—his great wealth—he never lost the habit of keeping a pile of the stuff handy in case of emergencies. Could be that he had some snide deal in mind that needed cash or negotiable bonds. At all events there was supposed to have been a lot of money in that house, and after Jacob's death none was found."

"This Walt Coburn," I said. "He must be right in the picture."

"I think he has a contact," said the Mouse readily. "The butler at Burnt Springs—Hubbard, his name is—"

"That guy again. Well, go on."

"The family discussed the money very excitedly. The general opinion was that Genevieve had cottoned on to it."

"Maybe she did."

"When they started saying there was a hook-up between Genevieve and that New York detective, Larry Kent, I figured it was time that Larry Kent was put wise."

I said nothing.

She twisted round so she could look up into my face. "Well, aren't you flattered?"

"Uh-huh."

"You might at least sound excited."

"I'm a suspicious guy," I told her. "Last night you were all for Rod Delamore. This morning you've broken with him and you're running round here to put me wise. Okay, baby, what's the payoff?"

"I hate you," she said crossly. "You're spoiling everything."

I reached out, picked her up by the elbows, carried her across the room and put her back in the chair.

"Simmer down," I told her. "You're making with plenty of sense. You want to tell me the reasons why you came, great. If not, we'll skip it."

She looked up at me and beamed me a smile. "Now I like you again. Larry, I listened to a lot of the talk, then I got tired of it. You know how it is. I barged in there with the half-cold coffee and told them right out that I'd been listening. That caused a commotion, I can tell you." She laughed, showing her small white teeth. "Rod was mad at me, and how! As for the old lady, she looked at me like she'd be happy to put an ice-pick in my head. I figured it was time to leave and I was just on my way out when Rod caught up with me. He started making with very tough talk indeed and it was then that he told me that he wasn't interested in me any more—he as much as said he had bigger game in his sights. So I figured it was as good a time as any to tell him to go and get lost." She sighed. "But I'm not broken-hearted over it. I guess I had a sort of maternal feeling for Rod. You know how some women get, Larry?"

"You tell me."

"I get myself a guy like Rod Delamore, and figure he needs reforming and I'm just the girl to do it. Then there comes a time when you just can't be bothered reforming him, and I guess that's how I feel right now."

I gave her a fresh cigarette and lit it for her.

She went on. "I went home and had a little sleep, just enough to make me want more. I had some strong, black coffee and thought things over. Then I decided to come right over and see you. Crazy, huh?"

"Yeah," I said. "Crazy as hell."

I reached down and put my hands under her armpits and lifted her clear off the chair.

"You like carrying me around?" she murmured.

I said nothing.

Our lips met.

She grabbed me round the neck. She was one of those surprising dames. Just full of surprises. We broke clean. She curled herself up against me like a kitten.

She murmured, "Larry, is it still raining outside?"

"Yeah, I guess so."

"I hate getting wet!"

"Be my guest," I said.

6

Throw the ball my way

The Pacific Grill was crowded.

I found Vince Callendar waiting for me at a reserved table. His fingers were drumming nervously on the tablecloth. He glanced up quickly as I pulled out a chair and sat down.

"Thank heaven you got here," he said in a relieved tone. "I was starting to worry."

"Uh-huh." The waiter was hovering. I gave my order.

Callendar waited until he had gone, then blurted out, "I was starting to think Belasco had pulled you in again."

"Why would he?" I lit a cigarette.

"Just about anything could happen right now." He leaned forward eagerly. "Where you been, Larry? I've been waiting here all of an hour—"

"Yeah," I said. "I got caught up."

"Any new developments?"

I shrugged. "A million of them."

He snapped, "Meaning what?"

I said, "Quit acting nervous. You're like a guy sitting pat with four aces. And keep your voice down."

He screwed up his eyes and nodded his head slowly. "You're onto something Larry, I can sense it."

"Yeah," I said. "Like I said it before."

"Meaning?"

"Old man Troy had a million bucks in cash and negotiable bonds stashed away in that house."

I saw his eyes bulge.

"Now I know why Genevieve was so anxious to have the old guy knocked off."

"Genevieve!" he exclaimed, but he was keeping his voice down. "For Pete's sake put me wise, Larry. You owe me that much."

"Hold it," I told him. The waiter was back. As he withdrew I attacked my plate of oyster mornay and while I ate I talked. I told him just what had happened the night before, right from the time when Danny Hester's yeggs picked me up, through the happenings at the Burnt Springs home of Jacob Troy.

His eyes were on me the whole time as I talked but he didn't interrupt once, though the veins were standing out on his temples from the strain of having to keep quiet.

I wound up, "I played along with Genevieve because I figured that way I'd open up Danny Hester the way you wanted it done. You heard me back there in the D.A.'s office—I put the finger squarely on Hester. Not because I figured the cops would pull him in, but just to start the ball rolling. Maybe a few things are looking clearer to you, Callendar."

Vince Callendar nodded. He burst out in a low tone, "You sure believe in earning your retainer, Larry! At the same time you didn't have to push it this far. After all, Jacob Troy's murder altered everything. Take it from me, Huntsman won't be holding you to your contract as of now."

I shrugged and pushed away my heaped plate of empty shells. He'd eaten nothing and had a cup of untasted coffee beside him. I took out cigarettes and lit one.

I said, "I've got a date with Genevieve at a place called the Pelican. You know it?"

He wrinkled up his forehead, then nodded suddenly. "Roadhouse. Doesn't have a very good reputation. Larry, are you crazy?"

"I'm not going to walk in there like a patsy, if that's what you mean. In fact, I'm half hoping Hester himself will be there to keep the appointment."

"In that case we'll have a squad of cops there."

"Uh-uh." I shook my head. "You're jumping the gun, Callendar. I've got to satisfy my curiosity first. After that, the law can take over."

He stared at me for a moment and then, "Larry, if I didn't know you so well, I'd be tempted to think you were playing along with Genevieve for the sake of the fifty grand she offered you."

I nodded, "Wouldn't blame you for thinking that."

"You're not mad at me?"

"Why should I be? A lot of guys would do a lot of things for fifty g's—only right now I'm not in the market."

He leaned back in his chair. He said softly, "How in hell does Genevieve think she can get away with this? Any minute you could put the finger right on her—"

"Sure I could, but she figures that I'm one of those guys who'd take fifty thousand."

He nodded soberly. And then, "Another thing." He leaned forward sharply in his chair. "Do you realize what this means? You're the only guy on earth who knows just how Jacob Troy was killed and how you were framed to take the rap. What's to stop Danny Hester taking out insurance?"

"You mean—not trusting me to take the fifty grand and keep my mouth shut?" I shrugged again. "You could be right at that."

"In that case," insisted Callendar, "Hester will rub you out."

"I guess he'll try."

"You shouldn't be here, Larry. Dammit, you should be hiding out some place ..."

"Be your age," I told him. "I took a couple of precautions back there at the hotel just in case some of Hester's hoods took it into their heads to pick the lock of my hotel room and liquidate me while I was asleep. But apart from that I'm just taking things as they come. For instance— I've been asked around to talk things over with a guy in your trade, Callendar. Lawyer name of Walt Coburn. Know him?"

"Do I know him?" he said at once. He made a gesture of disgust. He picked up his coffee cup and set it down untasted. "He's as crooked as hell but—he's always had the inside running as far as Jacob Troy was concerned. What does he want to see you about?"

"He's playing along with the Delamore family right now. My guess is that Jacob Troy changed his will. Maybe he had a habit of changing it. Coburn would know about that. He also knew about the million dollars cash. It won't be around anymore, you can bet on that."

He said instantly, "You figure Hester has it?"

"Who else? Every safe has a key. Genevieve could get Jacob's keys easily enough. Maybe she had a duplicate cut. That safe would be rifled within minutes of Troy being shot down by Lardner." A thought hit me and I added, "That would explain the slight time-lag before the trouble broke last night. I was knocked out by that bullet, but I can't have been unconscious more than a few minutes. When I came to they hadn't even checked to see if I was alive. Hubbard had heard the shots, and that kind of blew the thing up in their faces. But they'd have had enough time to empty the safe and get Danny Hester out of the way with the contents."

Callendar's head was nodding. He said, "What's to stop Hester and Genevieve getting clear away with the million?"

"Nothing, I guess. But don't forget Danny Hester isn't just a little guy who's suddenly tumbled into a pile of dough. He's got connections. He's got a growing empire. He's got real estate and he's got gambling tie-ups, liquor concessions with places like the Santa Rosa. He wouldn't just throw it up overnight."

"If the heat increases he'll just have to run for it."

"Maybe," I said, "and that could be why Genevieve wants to see me—just to make sure she can buy my silence."

"You figure she'll have fifty grand waiting for you at the Pelican?" Callendar asked incredulously.

"It isn't likely."

"But she'll have to make some sort of show of squaring off, or maybe it could be a trap with Hester sitting in. They'd pull anything, even in broad daylight."

I let smoke trickle in silence for a moment and then, "Get one thing clear, Callendar. Their plans have gone cockeyed through using me as the patsy. They don't know how much I've spilled to the cops—but they'll be guessing plenty. Now the cops are hunting Hester, the wires'll be humming and—Hester and Genevieve will be doing some pretty hard thinking."

I called for the check and paid the bill. We went out on the sidewalk.

Callendar said nervously, "I hate like hell you walking around loose like this."

"I'm a loose guy," I told him. I started to turn away when he grabbed at my arm.

"One thing, Larry."

"Yeah?"

"About this Walt "Coburn. I guess I should handle him."

I shook my head. "Leave him with me."

"And the Delamore family?"

Maybe I smiled. "Mildred Delamore and old man Willard Troy, and the youngsters—why, they're just breaking their necks to smear Genevieve and have themselves a slice of the Troy fortune. Whichever way the will breaks, I guess the Delamores are waiting like buzzards for their pickings, and the key to all that is Walt Coburn."

I checked the office in the directory and made the call. Coburn's voice came down the wire right away. "Larry Kent? Delighted to hear from you. Can you come round?"

"Sure."

"I'm on my own at present. You'll find me on the fourth floor—quite easy to locate. Say in a half hour?"

"Right away," I told him.

He hesitated and then, "I'm expecting another client any minute. I'd prefer to make it a half-hour, Mr. Kent."

"Okay," I told him and hung up.

I went and had myself a drink, then headed downtown for the building in which Coburn's office was situated. I was a quarter-hour ahead of time, but I had a hunch that it might be smart to look Coburn's set-up over before I was officially due to arrive.

Instead of riding up in the elevator I climbed the stairs. It was a quiet building tenanted by off-beat importers' offices, tailors, agents of all kinds. The lights were on even at that time of day, but it was still raining outside and the atmosphere was murky.

I found an indicator board with an arrow pointing to Coburn's office.

I walked down the corridor and reached the main door. It was standing open a little. I moved inside, and found myself in a cramped reception office. It was empty. And then I heard Coburn's voice from the other side of the far door. It was raised in anger.

"... and that's my last word on it! You can't bluff me that way, you young squirt! I'm not scared of you!" I heard Coburn give an angry laugh. "Why if it hadn't been for me, you and that precious mother of yours wouldn't have had a clue about Jacob Troy's affairs."

A voice mumbled in reply but I couldn't make out the words. I didn't have to be clairvoyant to guess that Coburn's client was young Rod Delamore, the Mouse's ex-boyfriend, the guy with the permanent thirst.

Coburn was ranting again, "I'm not going to be pushed around by you or any other member of your family. If I knew where Troy's will was, I'd have it out like a shot. Why would I cover up?"

I heard Rod say, "You double-crosser—"

"Don't you talk to me that way: I've had just about all I can stand of you, young Delamore. Now get the hell out of my office. In future I'll do business only with your mother or with your Uncle Willard. You keep out of this, you hear me? Keep out—"

His voice was choked off. There seemed to be silence for a little time, then a curious bumping noise.

I took quick strides to the door. I turned the handle but it was locked on the other side. I took out my gun, reversed it, smashed the butt against the panel above the latch. As it splintered I thrust my hand through and fumbled for the catch on the Yale, snapped it and pushed the door open.

Rod Delamore had wheeled round to face the door. His pudgy face was dead white, his eyes wild. In his right hand he held a heavy brass paperweight.

And sprawled on the carpet beside his desk was a little dark guy. He was spread-eagled and the top of his head wasn't pretty.

I said, "Okay, Delamore, drop that and put up your hands."

For a drawn-out minute I thought he was going to throw the paperweight at me, but he changed his mind and let it drop to the carpet with a heavy thud. He started to raise his hands, then said thickly, "This is crazy. You're not a cop. You can't make me do anything."

"Try me," I said. I went over to him, put out a hand and slammed him against the desk. His eyes were crazier than ever. With my free hand I roughly smacked him down to see if he was carrying a gun, but he wasn't. I grabbed him again, wheeled him off the desk and slammed him up against the wall so he bounced.

"Okay," I said. "What've you got to say before I call the cops?"

He laughed. "You won't be calling any cops, Kent."

"Uh-huh?"

"You don't have to look so surprised, either. You're in this as deep as I am."

I glanced at the figure on the carpet. "Coburn?"

"Who do you think?"

"You made quite a job of this guy." I dropped on one knee beside Coburn and then glanced up at Delamore. "Stay right where you are, brother, or I'll put another hole in your head."

I took a quick look at Coburn. He didn't even have a feeble pulse—he didn't have a pulse at all.

I got to my feet. I said, "Do they give guys the hot squat in this State or do they hang them?"

Delamore licked his lips. "Look, Kent, I killed him, sure. He attacked me. It was self defense."

"Uh-huh?"

"We were quarrelling over—" He stopped, then he shrugged. "You know what."

"You tell me, huh?"

"What's it matter? I guess we're all after Uncle Jacob's money."

"You figured that Coburn had it and was holding out on you?"

He laughed crazily. "Are you kidding? Coburn's only use to me was that he knew where Uncle Jacob had put his last will and testament. Uncle Jacob was the kind of guy always making new wills. Coburn knew that. He drew up most of them. I guess in latter months he fell foul of the old man and wasn't all that popular any more. But still he knew where that will was all right. He was holding out on me" Spitefully he lashed out with his foot at the prone body but didn't make it.

I said, "Ease down, Delamore. I heard what was said while I was standing out there. If he attacked you he must have used radar. It was clear cut homicide and you won't talk your way out of that one."

He was starting to shake a little. He wet his mouth again and then said, "See here, you're in on this. You've got to help me—"

"I can also help you go to hell."

"Rod!"

I whirled. Someone had rushed in the door—a dame with a slicker trailing over her arm, the other hand outstretched with a purse in it. Her hair was a blonde cloud, her complexion was peaches and cream.

"Angel," cried Delamore, and the dame stopped short.

I saw her lips were quivering. "Rod! What happened? What in heaven's name have you done?"

I said, "Lady, he just slugged your family lawyer. You better wait outside, huh?"

She looked at me. Her large violet eyes, were dewy with unshed tears. She gave a sob and suddenly threw herself right on my chest. I felt soft arms wound round me. She was all woman that dame, and for a couple of moments I forgot that she was supposed to be an up and coming actress in the movie world.

It was those couple of moments that cost me my gun.

She was smothering me.

I said, "Lay off, lady. Take it easy, can't you—" I tried to stall her off but she had more arms than an octopus. I got a mouthful of her hair, her whole body was pressed against mine. Sobs racked her. "Take it easy, can't you?" I stepped back and the next instant I felt the gun wrenched from my fingers. I jumped clear then and swung to face Rod Delamore, but he was crouched at the desk, my gun held in both hands.

He said through his teeth, "Don't move! Don't move or I'll drill you!"

"You think I'm crazy?"

I stood very still and Delamore said, "Good work, sis. You sure put over an academy winner that time."

Angel Delamore laughed.

I couldn't help looking at her. She was patting her hair into place. There wasn't a sign of stress on her face, and there certainly weren't any tears in those dewy eyes.

I said, "Congratulations," but she didn't even notice me. She stared down at the body on the floor then looked at her brother and said, "Rod, did you have to do that?"

"Yes," he replied, not taking his eyes off me. "He was—difficult then he threatened me. I—I guess I went crazy for a moment. You know what my temper's like."

"Yes, darling," said Angel. "But really, it was a little drastic, wasn't it?"

"Yeah," I said. "The law might figure he took it a little far."

She looked at me then. She said with contempt in her voice, "So you're Larry Kent. I heard about you."

"You won't be hearing much more about him," said Rod Delamore. "Angel, something's got to be done with this guy. He's leaning on us."

I said, "You're talking like a gangster, Delamore, and a tinhorn one at that. Get wise to yourself. You're out of your league, son."

I saw the gun jerk in his hand and he said loudly, "Don't lean too far, shamus, or by hell I'll blow your spine out."

Angel ran to him then and clutched to his arm. "Please, Rod, please. You're letting yourself get too excited."

"Yeah," I said. "How excited can you get?"

Then the telephone started ringing.

Nobody did anything, and then Rod jerked out, "Leave it ring! Leave it ring!"

It seemed to go on ringing a long time, then stopped.

Angel said rapidly, "Rod, I've got the car outside. We could take Kent down to the car and drive out home, then decide what we're going to do with him."

I said, "You're wasting your time. The way I'm fixed in this town I couldn't move a muscle without it being known down at Police Headquarters."

"He's lying," said Rod shrilly. "Don't take any notice of him, sis."

Angel Delamore walked right up to me, taking care not to get between me and her brother's gun. "Just where do you fit into this?"

"I could say the same about you."

She gave a short laugh. "Obviously I've got to back up my brother."

"Even in homicide?"

She closed her eyes for a moment and then opened them again. "I didn't reckon on this," she admitted. "I came in quietly and heard you talking, and then I saw what had happened."

"It's going to look great on the broadsheets," I told her. "Headlines on a movie actress mixed up in her brother's slaying charge—"

"There'll be no charges." Delamore's voice was shrill. "Nobody's going to find out about this. I'll tell you why, Kent. You'll never live to spill it." As he talked, Angel was staring into my face and I into hers.

I saw the changed expression come into her eyes. I knew for the first time she'd quit being an actress, backing up her brother in an exciting murder play. I said quietly, "Those headlines are for real, baby. You're not only out of your league, but way out of this world."

In a quick, excited tone of voice she said, "Surely there's some way out of this. Rod didn't mean to do it—if he makes a full confession—"

"Like hell I will." He came storming up, thrust her to one side and rammed the gun into my stomach. "You're going with us, Kent, right out there to my mother's house at Bel-Air. She'll know what to do with you."

I nodded. "I guess she wouldn't stop at murder to get her hands on Jacob Troy's dough, but—before we take off, you might as well know that that million dollars in loose cash isn't drifting around the Burnt Springs home any more. And as for Troy's estate I guess the last people on earth to benefit are the Delamores."

"He's right, you know, Rod," said Angel coolly. "Right through I've told mother that she's crazy even to hope to benefit—"

But again her brother wouldn't let her talk. He raged at me, "Why don't you mind your own affairs? We're doing this our way. We don't want any interference from you."

"Okay." I shrugged. "I just threw it in." I added, "Your move, buddy."

For a moment he looked at a loss; then he backed the gun away from me and said, "Turn round. Go on, turn."

"Have it your way," I told him.

I moved carefully. I wasn't fooling with that crazy guy, loaded as he was.

"Now walk out the door. Angel, you go first and see if the corridor's clear."

"Rod, I still think—"

"Do like I tell you."

She sighed. "Very well." She went out and I walked after her and Rod Delamore came behind, the gun brushing the back of my coat.

The corridor was clear, the elevator was on automatic and we rode down to the ground floor. On the way down Delamore pushed the gun into his side pocket and held on to it, the muzzle jutting my way.

"I guess we can get to the car without anybody noticing." His lips were peeled back off his teeth.

It struck me, looking at him, that it must have been a long time since he had his last drink. I figured that he must be pretty nearly at breaking point for want of it.

As we stepped out into the lobby, a couple of guys headed toward the elevator.

Delamore said, "You call out and it'll be the last sound you make."

Angel turned her head quickly but she said nothing, and kept on walking rapidly across toward the street doors. I followed, with Delamore right on my heels. We went down the steps, across the sidewalk and there was Angel tugging open the door of a convertible. She tipped forward the front seat and stepped back.

"In you get," snapped Delamore, and I crawled in and flopped back on the seat. I was half hoping Angel would share that snug seat with me, but instead she got up front, back of the wheel. Beside her Delamore crouched, half leaning over the seat, with the gun masked by his coat sleeve, pointed directly at me.

I said, "You qualifying for an academy award, too, Delamore?"

But he made no reply. He wasn't to be needled. His face was set like a mask.

Angel Delamore drove the convertible swiftly through the thick downtown traffic and headed out toward Hollywood.

Nothing was said, but I for my part, was thinking about Genevieve Troy and the date I was supposed to have kept with her at noon.

***

Angel swung the convertible off the road, through a pair of modest gates. Out the corner of my eye I saw the ordinary-looking black sedan, with the unobtrusive radio aerial, slide past us quietly. That black sedan had tailed us all the way from town, but neither Angel nor her brother had guessed it—Angel, for her part, intent on her driving, not aware of the need to look in the rear mirror—and as for Delamore, he had been so wrapped up in keeping that gun on me he hadn't had time for anything else.

I'd been half-joking back there when I'd warned them that the Police Department had more than a passing interest in my movements. Twice that morning I'd been aware there was a tail on me—on one occasion I felt reasonably sure I'd slipped him. That was when I was making my way from the Pacific Grill to the cross-town bar where I'd had a quick drink. I was plenty sure in my mind that the black sedan was a Police Department squad car, carrying civilian plates. It had picked us up either right outside Walt Coburn's office block, or shortly afterward.

Which argued that if the cops were in the vicinity, they could by how have discovered Coburn's body and the wires would be screaming any minute.

And then again, in an obscure block like Coburn's with furtive tenants minding their own affairs, the body might remain there all week—for I reminded myself that that day was Saturday.

I didn't have any more time for speculation. Angel had pulled the convertible to a stop with a jerk, right outside the villa. It was set among trees and had once been the home of a noted silent screen star in the twenties, and been bought for a song by the late A. K. Delamore.

"Get out first, Angel," said Rod, still not changing his position. "Get in there and tell mother what's happened."

Angel got out of the car, but reluctantly. She started to move away then changed her mind and came back, thrust her head in the side and said, "Rod—Rod darling—how does one explain a murder?"

"It wasn't murder, damn you." He whipped round to face her. "Tell mother I had a quarrel with Coburn, we fought and—and well, I hit him harder than I intended."

"I guess so."

"Are you losing your nerve? What's wrong with you? Go and tell mother and have her fetch Uncle Willard."

"Who's taking my name in vain?" broke in a voice.

I glanced past Angel and saw the stooped figure of an old guy standing on the driveway. His hands were thrust deep in the side pockets of his black weather coat, although the rain had stopped some time back. His bald head emerged incongruously from the high collar of his coat, and his big nose seemed to curve over his top lip. He had a big, booming nasal voice and he said, "What is this, Rod. What's the trouble?"

"Come here, Uncle, quickly."

Willard Troy started to come toward the car.

It was then that I figured it was time I got into the act.

Rod Delamore was half-kneeling on the front seat, his right arm across the back, the hand holding the gun drooping a little. His head was turned squarely to face his sister and Willard Troy beyond.

I knew my move would have to be fast—I wouldn't have time for two.

I swept my left hand up and sideways, cracking it into Delamore's gun hand. He must have had the safety catch thumbed back and his forefinger on the trigger, for the gun boomed at once, and the slug buried itself in the upholstery not all that far from my head. Then I had both hands on his wrist and was bearing down on it. He was arched like a bow across the back of the seat, and he started to scream like an animal.

I glanced up at the white frightened face of the dame at the window.

I said, "I'm taking my gun back, Angel. You want that I use it on your brother?"

She backed suddenly from the car.

"Hold it right there," I told her, and she stopped. Then I wrenched the gun from Delamore's fingers. He was still making a noise in his throat. Stretching his arm right down I twitched the gun round in my hand and slammed him across the side of the head with it. He slumped.

I kicked the driver's seat forward, slid out feet first. As I jumped onto the gravel I saw old man Willard Troy coming toward me with a rock in both hands. He had it poised, ready to toss it.

I said, "Don't do that, buster." I fired at the rock and it smashed to smithereens between his hands. Some of the flying stone must have penetrated his eyes, for he tumbled over with a yelping sound, and wrapped his arms about his head. He crouched there whimpering.

I said, "That leaves only you, Angel."

"You're wrong," boomed a voice from the ground floor window. "Put down that gun or I'll shoot you."

It sure was my day of surprises.

I caught a fleeting glimpse of an iron-gray head poking from the casement window. I thought of Barbara Frietchie and the march on Maryland. And Old Glory. And on my life insurance policy.

Because that old dame had a smooth-bore scatter-gun in her hands and it was leveled right on me.

I heard Angel scream, "Mother, be careful!"

I didn't wait to see if mother was careful or not. I fired at the window close to her head and saw her duck. Then I jumped back into the car, flicked on the ignition and backed the car down the drive about twenty yards. Then I swung hard on the wheel, slewed it round in a spatter of flying gravel and went charging back again.

The scatter-gun boomed from the window. I saw frightened birds go screaming out of the trees that lay between the house and the highway. That area was populated by folks in the high-income bracket; I guess it was the first time in years that a scatter-gun had blasted that prim silence.

I figured it would take Mildred Delamore some time to load that deadly pop-gun of hers. I braked the convertible to a stop, reached over and opened the far door, then thrust Red Delamore out on to the driveway. He started to jam in the doorway and I used my foot and kicked him clear through. Then I slammed the door and jerked the convertible into low and was just about to take off when the door was plucked open again and Angel flung herself into the car.

"Take me with you, Larry!"

I gunned the convertible down the drive. Without turning my head I said, "You don't get out of it this easy, baby."

I swung the car onto the highway. There was a scream of brakes and I glanced quickly around to see the black patrol bouncing to a stop. It had its nose headed for the entrance gate to the Delamore place. I had a glimpse of cops' faces glaring, then I took off down the hill and showed the patrol car my dust—the refined kind of dust they use around Bel-Air.

Beside me the dame said nothing until I'd swung the convertible around the corner, travelled a block, turned another corner fast; then she said, "I want to run away with you, Larry Kent."

"I'm not running any place."

"You don't look like it!"

"This is just a stall," I told her. "Right now I don't want to have to answer questions the cops might poke at me. After that, your guess is as good as mine, baby." I glanced in the rear vision mirror and saw the black car had been trapped at traffic lights. I said, "You take over, baby."

The traffic was thicker. I swooped in and out and then braked to a hard stop. I snapped open the door and slid out from back of the wheel.

"It's all yours," I told her.

She stared at me.

I said, "Beat it out of here fast."

With a convulsive movement she got behind the wheel. I dived through passers-by, scattering them, and headed for the open door of a drugstore. Just inside, I checked and looked out. Angel was playing along, or maybe it was just that she was so damned scared, flight was the only thing left to her. The convertible was gone and a second later the black police car fled past, hot on the trail. I eased myself into the phone booth, used nickels and called the District Attorney's office.

7

Stormy weather ...

Belasco came on right away. When I'd identified myself he said sharply, "Where are you, Kent?"

"Downtown."

"Not good enough. See here, you're not playing it smart. Isles and his homicide boys are getting madder every minute. They don't like playing tag around the city with a guy they want to finger for a murder."

"It's good practice for them," I told him. "Say, you located Danny Hester yet?"

"No, we haven't."

"Too bad you didn't put up real dough on that bet of yours."

"All bets off," he said, but there was no rancor in his voice. "As a matter of fact we pulled in one of Hester's henchmen—Nick Pullen."

"The twister? Well, isn't that too bad."

"Yeah," said Belasco. "Only Pullen isn't going to be much use to us. He's talked plenty but there's nothing we didn't know before. I guess he's conveniently forgetting the vital parts."

"Got any lead on Hester at all?"

"Not so far. Have you?"

"Are you kidding? I've got my worries, with Isles breathing down my neck." I wondered how far Angel Delamore had been able to go before the cops ran her into the gutter. I said, "I'll be keeping contact, Belasco."

He said sharply, "Now hold it right there. You heard anything from

Genevieve Troy?"

"No."

"She's disappeared, too."

"Funny coincidence."

"All airports and highways are being checked," said Belasco grimly. "If either of them try to get through, it's going to be just too bad."

"Either or together, huh?"

"Is that the way it is, Kent?"

I said, "Maybe if I get around to it I'll tell you a bedtime story some time."

Belasco said, "Now's as good a time as any." His tone was easy and amiable and suddenly it hit me: Belasco was nobody's fool. While he talked to me he had got through to one of his men and my phone call was being checked and located. Any minute now ...

I said, "Be seeing you, Belasco."

I hung up fast, walked quickly through the drugstore, out onto the street. I didn't fool around any out there. I got a taxi on the corner and told the hackie to take me to the Sheridan Hotel and halfway there said I'd changed my mind and paid him off.

I took another taxi and drove to a car-rent depot. Whilst they were running out a Ford for me and checking my out-of-State license number, I asked to use the telephone and they indicated one in the corner of the office.

I got through to Callendar's office right away. When Vince came on he sounded excited.

"Something new turned up! I just got the buzz from a friend of mine at City Hall. The D.A.'s office turned up Jacob Troy's last will and testament—dated only a few days ago."

"No kidding."

"My information is that Jacob Troy left the bulk of his estate to a California Foundation for the Care and Welfare of Orphans. How do you like that, Larry?"

"That Jacob Troy," I said, "sure had a sense of humor." I added, "Looks like brother Willard and the Delamore family are left out on a limb."

"Yeah," said Callendar and chuckled. "Say, Larry, where are you, for Pete's sake?"

"Drifting around," I told him. "Look, you can do something for me."

"Anything."

"Go round to the D.A.'s office and tell him Troy's attorney, Walt Coburn, was killed in his office today."

"Killed!" exclaimed Callendar. "Who in hell—"

"Rod Delamore beat him over the head with a brass paperweight. The D.A. will find the body right there in Coburn's office—that is unless the cops haven't already caught up. Put it on the line for him, Callendar, and tell him I was right outside the door when it happened. Also, Angel Delamore's in the clear. She got there long after it happened."

"Look, Larry, what's all this add up to?"

"Mayhem," I told him.

I hung up.

***

It was late in the afternoon.

There weren't many houses around the area where the Pelican roadhouse was situated. I drove clear past the place, giving it a quick once-over. I didn't slow. I drove right up the hill, then turned and headed back again. When I was four hundred yards from the place I ran the rented car down a dirt road, branched off that and bumped over rough ground until I could go no further. I climbed out, detached the ignition key, dropped it in my pocket. I headed for the dirt road, then looked back. The rear of the car could just be seen but it must have been invisible to anybody on the highway.

Keeping off that highway I made my way down the hill until I came to a fence. I crawled through, then paused, looking about me.

The roadhouse was right ahead. It was built of pink stucco on sham Moorish lines. There seemed to be outbuildings—a chicken run, trees standing thickly about. There seemed to be no sign of life around the place.

I made a half circuit of the roadhouse without seeing anybody or anything suspicious. There was one car parked in the short driveway to the side of the main building, but it had its bonnet up as if somebody had been fooling with the motor. From the inside of the house came the sound of a telephone ringing, then it stopped, and I could hear a muffled voice talking.

Peaceful, and apparently, as harmless as a Sunday school picnic.

I still wasn't satisfied. If Genevieve Troy had kept the appointment she must have gone long since. And then again if she was double-crossing me, she must have had Hester, or some of Hester's hoods with her. It wasn't likely that she would just come here, wait awhile, then go away again.

That is, if there were to be a double-cross.

I was lying in thick brush not twenty yards from the side of the house. I raised myself on my elbows and stared across at another patch of brush that faced the drive-in from the highway.

Then I saw it again—a flick of light—the merest flash, like something had been caught in the sun and reflected briefly. Something moving.

I watched for a while longer. Again there was that flash. Cautiously I wriggled back, stood upright, moved around the fence and cut back into the second patch of brush. I moved lightly, making no sound.

And then I saw him. He was lying on his stomach on a mound of dirt that was for all the world like an old grave. Grass grew thickly about it and the place was screened by stunted brush and a few tall trees. The guy was lying very still except that he was smoking and every now and then he would raise his right arm, taking the cigarette from his mouth and putting it back away. As he did so the sun caught the metal bracelet of his wristwatch and it was that flash I had seen back there.

I stood and watched him.

I couldn't see his face, but there was something familiar about that guy ... He must have sensed something, maybe my intent gaze. He suddenly plucked the cigarette from his mouth and ground it out in the earth beside him. Then he drew his legs up and I knew he was going to stand. I moved quickly to one side, drawing my gun. The guy was getting to his feet. He turned round casually—and the next instant saw me, and I saw him clearly, too—Al Lardner.

He was fast on his reflexes, faster than I had figured he would be. He snapped up his gun and fired. The bullet chopped twigs from the branch close to my face. I dodged sideways into the brush, tripped and all but fell. I heard Lardner give an exultant whoop and come crashing toward me. I snapped upright and swung my .32 round.

"Come into my parlor," sang out Lardner. "Come right on in, shamus."

And then he was there, only a few feet away. He was grinning. Again his gun came up, but I snapped the .32 at him and by the time his gun exploded he was dead.

I looked down at him. For the first time, No-Face Lardner had really lived up to his name.

***

The guy with the blue chin stood in the roadhouse patio.

He had his hands high above his head, and his jowls were quivering.

I said, "Take it easy and nobody's going to get hurt." I leaned against the door frame, gun slanting on him. "Who else is here with you?"

With difficulty he mouthed, "Two—man and wife—out back."

"Why didn't they show?"

"Guess they was too scared to move, mister."

I nodded. "Who came here today besides that guy out there?"

"I don't know, mister—" Then he gave a sharp intake of breath as I jabbed the gun in his direction. "Don't shoot. I should worry about Danny Hester. He was here, for sure. And the dame. There was a dame. Tall, blonde—that's right, mister. She came first. She waited out here on the patio. She waited around an hour. Then Danny Hester showed up. They had drinks. They talked and then the lady, she went away in her auto."

"And Hester?"

"He went away, too, mister."

"In his auto?"

"No, on foot."

I stared at him. "And the other guy?"

"There was two others. One stayed behind to watch the drive-in. The other went away with Hester."

I nodded again. "Okay," I said. "If Hester gets back, tell him I've been." I backed out.

The sun was slanting down as I made my way up the hill toward where I had parked my car. But I went past the turn-off to the dirt road and climbed right to the top of the hill. It was worrying me that Hester had gone and yet there had been no car. There just had to be a car—Hester wasn't moving around California on foot. Not with all the cops in Los Angeles looking for him.

There was a clear space at the top. I crossed it and looked down the other side of the hill. I could see the gleam of a roof through the trees, and a half-mile the other way another roof. Then I heard the drone of a car speeding down the highway: the sound was soon lost, then silence.

I picked my way back across the clearing. I figured my hunch must have gone haywire.

Then I stopped suddenly.

There was a gleam through the trees to my right. At first I thought it was the roof of a house, then when I looked more closely I saw that it couldn't be.

I moved closer, making my way from tree to tree, stepping lightly.

And then I was close to it and I saw it was a trailer.

Danny Hester's trailer.

***

It stood there in a clear space in the woods, and I could see the tire marks leading in and out, zigzagging down the slope to pick up the dirt road on which I'd parked my own car. I drew closer. It was very quiet in there. The trailer stood forlornly, as if deserted. There was no towing car with it. There was no sound except the chattering of a squirrel way up in a tree close by.

I snicked back the safety catch of my .32 and edged round the clearing until I had a view of the trailer door. It was hooked back and the interior seemed dark, full of menace.

I waited.

The other guy cracked first.

There was a sudden snapping of twigs, and the guy rushed out from the other side of the clearing. He had a sub-machine gun held high in his arms. I had a momentary glimpse of his face—a little fat guy with hard eyes. Then I was swinging up my automatic.

"Hold it right there," I called.

But he came on. Maybe the quiet of that place had needled his nerves—he must have had a long wait. He snapped the sub-machine gun down to his hip. I saw his hand working. I shot him in the hand. But that didn't stop him, either. He threw himself headlong, jerked the Thompson into position. I could hear him cursing me. I threw myself to one side and fired. The sound of my gun was lost in the appalling clatter of the machine gun. The air seemed to be full of screaming lead and flying chips as the bullets tore their way through the brush.

I took deliberate aim, squeezed the trigger three times.

The firing stopped abruptly.

I walked over to the fat guy. He'd rolled over on his side. The Thompson had fallen away from him. He was very dead.

I climbed into the trailer, looked around. It was just like it had been the night before, only there was no Danny Hester—no Al Lardner.

I went back out into the golden sunlight of the dying afternoon. I picked up the machine gun and carried it to the brush and dumped it. Then I went back to the little guy, grabbed him and dragged him across the clearing and dumped him, too. I went back and kicked the dirt around, then climbed into the trailer.

I poured myself a bourbon from the tiny drink-closet, then took the spare clip of shells from my side pocket, replaced the depleted one in my gun. I dropped the .32 into my shoulder holster, sat down on the davenport and waited.

Danny Hester just had to come back.

**

He came back when the sun had gone and a light breeze was rustling the tops of the trees around that clearing. I heard the motor first, but I had heard plenty of traffic running spasmodically along the highway a half-mile away. But then I saw headlights spearing the dusk, vanishing, returning as the approaching car dodged in and out among the trees.

I went into the shower recess and cramped myself against the wall, took out my gun.

I heard the car coming whining in on second gear. The headlights swept across the trailer briefly and then I heard the auto being backed. The motor was cut.

There was a pause and then I heard Danny Hester's voice calling sharply, "Henry—! Where in hell you got to?"

Another pause.

"Henry?" he called again and then cursed.

I heard him tramping into the trailer. He called again and his voice boomed through the trailer. Again he cursed. Then he went out, unhooked the trailer door and slammed it shut. I heard a clanking noise as he coupled the car to the trailer. Then the auto started up again. Slowly the trailer went into motion. It bumped and swayed down the hillside, turned sharply, ran a little more smoothly and then with a swoop we were on the concrete pavement and the trailer was running fast.

I moved out and made my way through to the drink closet and had myself another bourbon. It was getting that way I was starting to like the stuff.

The trailer ran smoothly on. I hoped we'd find Genevieve at the other end.

The last few miles had seemed rougher, as if he'd left the highway. I peered out one of the scuttles but could see nothing but a lot of blackness, no lights any place. I remembered California was quite a State, and only a few miles out of Los Angeles and the hard glitter of Hollywood, lay deserts and mountain ranges that could seem as isolated as the Grand Canyon.

I had myself another bourbon. I was getting bored with that trailer. I prowled around. Hester sure lived it up—had just about every comfort a guy would wish for in that mobile home. But I wasn't interested in luxuries right then. I pulled open the lockers beneath the davenport. One of them contained only unimportant details but the other held a black leather valise, strapped and double-locked. I hefted it out and dropped it on the davenport and stared at it.

The trailer seemed to be slowing.

I snapped open my knife and slit the bottom of the valise. It was tough going but at last I made it. I had that valise opened like an over-ripe orange.

And I was looking at a heap of U.S. cash money and the scrolled paper of negotiable bonds, scattered about that davenport.

We were bumping to a stop. I crammed the cash back into the valise, dropped it in the locker and slammed it shut. Then I went quickly back to the shower recess.

It was very quiet out there now we'd stopped. Then the trailer moved a little as the car was unhitched from it. I heard voices out there. Presently the trailer door was snapped open. I heard Hester's voice.

"Mrs. Troy got here yet?"

"Yep. About a half-hour back, Danny."

"Tell Cal to have the Cessna warmed up."

There was a further jumble of voices. I was trying to figure out "Cessna." And then I got it. A light aircraft, fast, easily piloted. Hester's escape hatch.

And then there was the sound of someone climbing into the trailer. The bulkhead lights were snapped on. I heard the locker beneath the davenport being opened and then—Danny Hester ripped out a curse. He must have jumped up fast and leapt out the trailer. I heard his raised voice calling. I moved after him. I dropped to the ground, edged my way round the back of the trailer and stopped.

It looked like a ranch-house, a low-lying, massive building with lights showing at ground level. I had the sensation that there was a lot of empty space all around—an out-of-town ranch for sure, with a convenient private airstrip for Hester's Cessna.

I saw a light bobbing away from the house and I remembered Hester's instructions to have the plane ready. Looked like I'd have to be fast.

I edged my way along the side of the house. There was a low wall. I climbed it and found myself on a sort of patio. There was an archway and I moved through. It was dark out there, but I could see a light a little ahead. I pushed at a door and found it locked. I moved further along, found a window and swung myself and used the blade of my knife to snap the catch. I eased myself into the room and headed for the light I'd seen through the transom.

Then I heard Danny Hester's voice. Sounded like he was raving.

I drew closer. There was a hallway and an open door beyond. I crossed the hall quickly, flattened myself against the wall.

Genevieve's voice came. "You must be crazy talking this way. I haven't been near the trailer. Why should I? It must have been one of the boys—"

"If it'd been one of the boys they'd have taken the cash. Somebody slit that briefcase wide open—" He broke off.

A telephone was ringing shrilly.

"Well, why don't you answer it?" Genevieve's voice was sharp.

I heard the receiver being taken up and Hester's curt tones as he answered the call. Then the receiver was put up fast. There was a slight pause and then in a deadly tone he said, "What do you know, baby. That was Omeo from the Pelican. Larry Kent's been there."

I heard Genevieve gasp, then Hester say, "He went there and he killed Al."

"Danny!"

"Looks like we should have taken care of that guy but good. You know what this means, baby? Omeo was so scared he could hardly talk, which means he'll talk plenty to the cops." As if a sudden thought hit him he added explosively, "Kent must have got to Henry, too. He'd disappeared when I reached the trailer—" He broke off. "The trailer," he said softly.

I could almost read his mind.

I eased myself around the door frame. I called out, "End of the line, Hester."

The two of them faced me. Genevieve's blonde hair wasn't smooth any more. Her eyes looked wild. Hester's mouth had opened a little. He stood as if frozen.

I took a step into the room. I stopped. I said, "You should have quit a long time back."

I couldn't be blamed for overlooking the third person in that room. He was standing over near the window and I hadn't heard him say a word when I'd been listening outside the door. I saw him now—too late. He plunged forward and his gun spat. I felt the slug tear into my left shoulder, and spun round. I fired and saw him keep on running, like he'd been hit from behind.

But I knew Danny Hester was going for his gun—even without looking I knew it.

And then as I staggered round to face him I heard Genevieve scream, "No, Danny, no!"

As if through a haze I saw her jump forward—getting between Hester's gun and me.

And in that instant he fired.

Genevieve was between us, all right, but she was clutching at her stomach with a surprised look on her face. She crumpled slowly, like a doll with the sawdust running out. And before she hit the floor I was on to Hester ... smothering his gun as he stood staring down at Genevieve with stark horror on his face. I took the gun from him easily. It was only then that he jerked up his head. He mouthed something at me. I hit him on the temple with the sights of his gun. He reached out hands, gibbering. I hit him again. He went down. He didn't move.

I went to the phone, picked it up wearily, and got through to the D.A.'s office. While I waited I nursed the phone against my wounded shoulder and held my gun slanted on the doorway. But nobody came—that is, nobody until the local cops came pouring in, three car-loads of them from Sarina. And they were just the beginning of it. Belasco sure put on a show that night, smashing the last of Danny Hester's empire.

And all the time I could see Genevieve's face, stricken, frozen in death.

***

I stood on the corner of Hollywood and Vine and watched the world go by.

Vincent Callendar found me there. "Figured you might be here."

"Yeah," I said. "As an out-of-State tourist I guess I owe it to myself to take in all Hollywood's got to offer."

He glanced at me. He was grinning a little. "How does the shoulder feel?"

"You've got good surgeons in L.A."

"How about giving me the bullet as a souvenir?" He chuckled.

I said, "You've sure got a Hollywood sense of humor."

We went to the nearest bar. As we sat on stools Callendar said, "When do you go back?"

"Tonight."

"Sorry to see you go, Larry."

"Uh-huh."

"You know, Jacob Troy's death triggered off a lot of things—Angel Delamore's had so much publicity these last few days she's been given a star part in a new movie."

"Great."

"Looks like her brother Rod will get off with a light sentence—maybe ten years in Alcatraz."

"That's too bad, too."

He chuckled as he raised his glass. "Well, here's to Jacob Troy." He drank.

I said, "Anything new from Belasco?"

He looked at me in surprise. "What could be new? The case is all sewn up—Danny Hester spilled all Belasco wanted to know in an oblique kind of way. Belasco's no fool. He can read lines into the dialogue that were never meant to be there. Well, Larry, this looks like so long."

"Yeah," I said. "And you owe me a thousand bucks, Callendar."

I briefly noticed the dame in the seat across the aisle. All I could see of her was her shoulder, her ear, and some of her brown hair. Even at that she looked cute. I got up and made my way down the aisle of the big Continental airliner to the bar. A stewardess gave me a smile as she fed me liquor.

"It's too bad having to leave the Sunshine State," she observed, friendly as hell.

"Sure," I said. "You know something, sister? I can hardly wait to see Manhattan's topless towers sticking out through the East River smog."

She laughed. "Well, it takes all kinds."

"Sure does." I went back to my seat and checked. It was occupied. By the little dame from across the aisle.

I said, "I didn't know you right off."

The Mouse smiled at me mischievously. "Hello, Larry."

I said, "Your hair—"

"I went back to mousey brown. Do you like it?"

"Well, it's different."

She laughed, "Just so long as you like it, Larry."

I said, "Going far?"

"Clear through to New York."

"Then it looks like we'll be together, Mouse."

"Clear through," she said.

HONEY-BLONDE BLUES

Larry Kent's old buddy Jim Calloway was murdered over a woman ... so they said. But who was the woman? No one seemed to know — not even Jim's killer.

Larry suspected the woman was just a diversion. There was another reason for Jim's death. And just maybe it had something to do with his job with the Narcotics Bureau. Only thing was, Jim was a minor official at the Bureau, no one with any clout, just a desk-jockey.

One thing for certain. There were people out there — important people — who wanted to bury the case. And if they couldn't kill Larry to stop him investigating, then just maybe they could send him to Cuba in search of a missing man. After all, he'd be easier to rub out in a foreign country ...

1

A guy only fries once ...

The guard nodded to me and I went through to the inner cell. I heard the outer door clang and glanced round to see the other guard sitting down again at the metal table, just inside the doorway.

A voice said, "Don't a guy get any privacy around here?"

Dan Harbin was sitting at a small table. There was a blanket folded over it. He had dealt out a hand of solitaire.

I said, "One question, Harbin."

No answer. He was grinning.

I said, "Who was Calloway's girlfriend?"

Harbin laughed. He said to the guard. "Who let this punk shamus in here?"

The guard said nothing. He was leaning against the wall with his arms folded.

I said, "Who was the dame, Harbin?"

He got up off his chair carefully, as if every move he made had to be deliberate, calculated—timed. He moved round the side of the little table and stood facing me, blocky, sandy-haired, his eyes empty, his mouth a sneer.

"You find out who she was, Kent. Me, I've got other things on my mind."

He struck without warning, a short chopping blow to the pit of my stomach. I swayed, jerked up my hands—and checked the punch. Harbin was screaming, "I'll kill ya, ya bum!"

Then the guard was between us. He fumbled his grip and Harbin all but got away from him. He was writhing like a madman. There was a dribble of saliva down his chin.

Then the other guard was running in, and I heard a clatter at the outer door. In a few seconds they had Harbin flat on his back on his cot. Over his shoulder the guard said breathlessly, "You better blow, Mr. Kent. Time's run out—"

I said, "For that guy, too."

I went out through the double doors. The deputy governor was waiting for me. He was frowning.

"I won't ask you how you made out—"

"No dice," I told him.

He nodded. "You better come back to the chief's office with me." As we walked along he glanced at his wrist, checked the time with the big clock at the end of the echoing hall.

"Thirty-five minutes to go," he said.

And when we were back in the executive offices I stood around and watched the urgent comings and goings—broken by a quick call from the District Attorney's office, countermanding his previous order that I be allowed to see the condemned man.

Deputy Randall hung up and gave me a crooked grin as he told me the news.

"The D.A. left his change of mind a little late."

"Yeah," I said. "Too bad about that."

I lit a fresh cigarette.

Then a bell started ringing some place—a long, insistent sound. I glanced at the deputy and saw a nerve twitching in his cheek.

Then on a wall panel near his desk a red light went on, held for a few seconds, went off again, then showed once more.

There was complete and utter silence in the room.

The red light went off. A green light showed.

And I saw the lamp over the deputy-governor's desk dim for a few seconds and then show bright again.

The guard standing stiffly at attention near the door relaxed suddenly and I saw him cross himself.

The deputy-governor said, "Now we'll never know why Harbin

killed James Calloway."

***

There was a bunch of newspapermen and photographers outside the tall gates of the penitentiary. I walked quickly over to my waiting taxi. I was all but there when I saw a guy detach himself from the car against which he had been leaning and start toward me. I had a glimpse of a thin face in the electrics that spilled over the driveway; above the face was a Panama hat with a faded red ribbon round it. As I dived into the cab I wondered fleetingly about that Panama hat; it looked out of character on a newsman covering a big shot's execution.

The taxi sped down the driveway and I lit a fresh cigarette, expecting the inevitable questions from the driver. But the hackie, his face lined and worldly wise, uttered not a word. I tipped him five bucks when we reached the railroad station and he nodded, still without speaking.

I made my way down the concourse, paused to buy a news magazine and a late edition of the *Clarion*. I had a few minutes to wait.

The *Clarion* had the last-minute news on Harbin, tucked away on page nine. The next edition would carry an even smaller paragraph, to the effect that Harbin had been duly executed, and "justice had been done."

I glanced over the brief story they ran on page nine of the edition: a terse recapitulation of the events that had led up to Harbin's trial for the murder of Jim Calloway.

The train slid in and I stepped on board. Something made me turn my head at the last moment, and I had a fleeting glimpse of the thin-faced guy in the Panama hat climbing into the train two coaches down. I shrugged and made my way through to a seat by the window, dropped my briefcase in the rack and stretched myself out comfortably. The coach was all but empty.

I finished reading the *Clarion's* story. They even had a plug for me.

"James Calloway was found shot dead on the night of June 19. The body was found by a patrolman just before midnight in an alley at the side of the Excelsior Club on Canal Street. There seemed to be no motive for the crime: Calloway was a minor official in the Narcotics Bureau and as far as police could determine had never had contact with members of the underworld. He was a war veteran who lived alone with his mother in a quiet park side apartment. He had few friends outside of his work and was believed to have had no enemies.

"At first it seemed there must be some connection between the shooting and the fact that Calloway was employed by the Narcotics Bureau. But the Bureau pointed out at the time that Calloway was not an outside operative but was employed purely as a desk executive at headquarters. There was nothing at all in his record to show that he had had any direct contact with the narcotics traffic. Due largely to the work of a city private investigator, Larry Kent, an important witness was turned up in the person of Whitey Gondola, a small-time mobster, who was once a triggerman for Duke Cerise. Although Gondola was able to prove an alibi, it was through him that the Homicide Bureau, again with the help of Kent, followed a lead that eventually brought Daniel Harbin to trial.

"New evidence came to light following the arrest of Harbin. It was proved that Calloway was not a regular frequenter of the Excelsior Club, and left the place alone on the night of the nineteenth and that Harbin who had been drinking with cronies, left almost immediately afterward. There was conflicting evidence from passers-by about a quarrel taking place in the opening to the lane alongside the club; at all events police were able to get a confession from Harbin who finally boasted that he had killed Calloway because of an argument over a girl. Attempts by the police to extract further details from Harbin have not been successful. Harbin was duly tried and found guilty..."

"Excuse me, Mr. Kent."

I glanced up. Sure enough it was the guy in the Panama hat. I said, "You got the wrong guy, buddy."

"I don't think so," said the Panama hat. He was standing there in the aisle between the seats, swaying slightly to the motion of the train. I could see that he was older than I'd thought and though his hat was shabby the rest of his clothes were not.

I said, "Beat it, I'm busy."

He didn't move. "I just want to talk with you, Mr. Kent. It'll only take a few minutes."

"I've got no minutes for the Press."

"Oh, but you have me wrong," said the thin guy quickly. "I'm not from a newspaper."

I looked at him. "Radio, maybe? Or one of those TV roundsmen with a cute little tape-recorder in your pocket?"

He smiled faintly and shook his head. "You've got me wrong. I'm just a private citizen, Mr. Kent and—I'd appreciate it if you'd give me a few minutes of your time."

"Talking about what? Executions, maybe?"

He shook his head. "Dan Harbin's dead. I would say, all round, a good thing."

"Sure," I said. "Read the obituaries tomorrow."

He put out a hand to steady himself as the train took a bend at high speed. He said, "My name's Jackson. I represent J. B. Weiler." Before I could speak he fished a card from a vest pocket and held it out to me.

I said, "Right now I'm stocked up with vacuum cleaners."

He licked his lips rapidly. "Mr. Kent; I'm not selling anything. I'm hiring."

I took out a package of cigarettes. As I shook one loose I said, "I'm not open for hire."

He blinked. "You *are* Larry Kent, aren't you? The private investigator?"

"Yeah," I said. "I just finished a tough case, and I'm taking a vacation."

"Perhaps J. B. Weiler could make you change your mind, Mr. Kent?"

"Nothing could." I shook out my copy of the *Clarion*, "See you, Jackson."

I started to read the sport page.

I knew he was still there.

"Mr. Kent?"

I said nothing.

He leaned closer to me. I could smell garlic faintly. In an earnest voice he said, "You still want to find out who Calloway's girl was?"

I threw the paper from me and got to my feet.

Jackson stood his ground.

I said, "What you trying to pull?"

"You've got me wrong, Mr. Kent. Maybe you've never heard of J. B. Weiler?"

When I said nothing he went on, "He's a very wealthy man—a rich importer of goods from Cuba. He asked me to contact you just as soon as this Harbin business was over—he's followed your progress quite keenly, Mr. Kent."

"Guess he had fun."

Jackson smiled faintly. "J. B. has contacts all over the city. Even in the police department. In fact, Captain Wagner who was in charge of the Calloway case is a good friend of his."

"So what?"

"Won't you talk with J. B. Weiler?"

"About what?"

"I think he'd prefer to tell you himself, Mr. Kent."

I said, "If it's a case, I'm not interested."

"Not even in—" He hesitated, "A five hundred dollar fee?"

"Usually," I told him. "But right now I'm through with work. See me in one month, Jackson." I sat down again and reached for my discarded paper.

The guy still didn't move. One stubborn guy. I ran my eye down the major league results. I heard Jackson say in his light, impersonal voice, "I've placed one of J. B.'s cards on the arm of your seat, Mr. Kent. If you change your mind in the morning, call him. He'd be very happy to see you anytime in the next twenty-four hours."

I dragged on my cigarette. Presently I turned my head. Jackson had gone.

***

At the terminus I was pushing my way through the crowd when I caught sight of the Panama hat just ahead of me, bobbing along among the commuters heading for the escalators. I had Weiler's visiting card in my side pocket. Then I lost sight of him altogether. It was on a higher level. I was walking past the corner of a news stand when it happened.

The crowd had lessened a lot but I was suddenly jostled—felt a thrust against my back and turned quickly to see Jackson's face peering at me anxiously. I started to say, "What in hell—" when he pushed me to one side violently.

I crashed against the corner of the news stand and swung round. I guess there was a savage look on my face—but I wiped it when I saw a guy standing not more than two feet away, stooped a little, with his right hand thrust out as if trying to shake hands.

Only a guy doesn't do that when he's got a naked blade in his hand.

I heard someone call out something and I surged forward. The guy with the knife seemed to bend his knees and jump sideways. He went through the crowd like a quarterback with the ball. In moments he was lost to sight.

I could see people looking at me curiously as I straightened my tie. I said, "Jackson, did you see that guy with the knife?"

"Why do you think I pushed you, Mr. Kent?"

"Thanks," I told him.

The look of nervousness on his face vanished. "I'm glad you're not sore at me. I was coming up to speak to you again—then I saw him. I figured the smartest thing to do would be to push you out of the way first and explain afterwards."

"It was smart," I told him. "Any time I need help of that kind I'll call you."

He said anxiously, "Mr. Kent, have you any idea who that man was?"

"I never saw him before in my life."

"Forgive me, but might he be a friend of Daniel Harbin's, perhaps?"

"Could be."

The commuters were streaming past us unconcernedly. The whole thing had happened so quickly it was as if only a tiny pebble had been thrown into a big, big pool.

Jackson said, "Maybe you need a change of climate, Mr. Kent. Why not take a working vacation? J. B. Weiler will pay well."

I said, "Look, Jackson, I owe you something for getting me out of the way of that knife, but I'm not working for Weiler now or any other time. You get it?"

He said, "Just as you say, Mr. Kent."

"Sure," I said. "Just like I say."

I was turning away when he said urgently, "Doesn't it even intrigue you?"

I looked at him. "Doesn't what intrigue me?"

"The fact that I asked you about the girl in the Calloway case?"

I said, "A salesman's got to use any lead he can think up when he's trying to swing a deal. Right, Jackson?"

"I think you've got me wrong, Mr. Kent."

"It's getting to be a habit with me," I told him. "See you around."

***

I had a Scotch uptown and took a cab round to Police Headquarters. Captain Wagner was on duty and I was admitted right away.

"Sit down there, Larry. I won't be a minute signing these."

I walked over to the window and looked out. From Wagner's office, high up in the building, Manhattan by night was laid out like a picture in a story book. That was the way it had to be; a cop's-eye view of a town where somebody died violently just about every hour of the day.

"So you went out after all to see Harbin burned?"

"I didn't watch." I swung round to face Wagner, who was sitting in his chair looking at me quizzically.

He nodded and said, "The deputy-governor called me. Sounds like you didn't get any last words out of Harbin."

"I wasted my time."

"I'm told he even attacked you in his cell?"

"Yeah," I said. "He handled me a little. Remind me to get this suit dry-cleaned, Wagner."

He said, "Do I have to tell you that the temperature in this town might go up for you, Larry?"

"I already noticed that."

His eyebrows went up.

I said, "When I got off the train I just missed being carved up by an eager guy."

Wagner exclaimed, "Right out there in the open?"

"Well, it was below street level—"

"You know what I mean," he said impatiently. He got to his feet and came round the side of the desk. "What happened, Larry?"

I told him briefly. I wound up, "The guy got away in the crowd and I didn't follow up. There wasn't any point in it. It was a lucky break."

"Yes," said Wagner and screwed up his eyes as he looked at me. "Maybe that's the red light you've been needing, Larry. When do you leave town?"

I laughed.

"Okay, so I'm wasting my breath telling you. But—this Calloway case has brought you a lot of publicity."

"Yeah," I said. "I read the *Clarion,* too. Good plug. Better than paid advertising."

"I'm serious," said Wagner and looked hard at me. "You've been more in the public eye over this case than any other I can remember. I guess just about every newspaper reader and TV viewer knows by now that Calloway was a buddy of yours in the Pacific during the war. That you took a personal interest in the case and—well, you got his killer."

"I helped," I told him. I took out a cigarette and lit it. "I'm not looking for any cheap halos nor bouquets from the Police Department. For the record, I'm not all that interested in anything Harbin's friends might do. That is, unless they pull something that gives me the answer to the question I threw at Harbin before they fried him."

"About the girl?"

"Sure." I dragged at my cigarette, watching him. "I knew Jim Calloway pretty well. He was one straight-shooting guy. Naturally I didn't know everything about his private life. What he didn't tell me I didn't ask about. One thing I do know—he wasn't the type to feud with a cheap mobster like Harbin over a girl."

"We know that," said Wagner abruptly. "The homicide detail worked for six weeks trying to open up the real motive for Harbin killing Calloway the way he did. We found nothing and Harbin wouldn't talk. Well, justice has been done, as the good books say. Harbin's dead and we'll maybe never know if there was a girl in the case at all—"

"I think there was," I broke in.

He said quietly, "You got some inside dope, Larry?"

"No." I shook my head. "I'm not holding out on you. I listened to Harbin's testimony and I read the statements that he made to the police, after his arrest. I think he was telling the truth about some things and—there *was* a girl some place in the background. Maybe it's just that I want to clear Calloway's memory—or even satisfy my own curiosity—whatever the hell it is, I want to know who that girl was, and why Calloway was killed."

Wagner nodded and moved back to his chair. "Okay, so you won't be scared out of New York. Will you take a little fatherly advice?"

"Go right ahead, pappy." I must have grinned as I ashed my cigarette in his tray.

He said, "You're looking tired."

"It's been a tough case."

"Maybe because Calloway was a personal friend of yours—" He held up his hands and dropped them again.

"It's all over now. I advise you to go take a trip some place."

"I intend to," I told him.

"Now, that's better," he said in a relieved tone of voice. "Go some place nice and quiet and sit in the sun and do some fishing."

"Yeah," I said. "I'll check through my little black book when I get home tonight. There's a dame I've been fishing for for years—"

"All right," sighed Wagner. "Play it your way, only when you come back to town don't have those bags under your eyes. They depress me."

I mashed out my cigarette. I said, "Wagner, tell me something before I go?"

"What is it?"

"Who's J. B. Weiler?"

He was silent for a moment and I said, "It's claimed he's a personal friend of yours."

"No," said Wagner. "Not that, but I know him. He's quite a big shot."

"Uh-huh?"

"What you want to know about him, Larry?"

"Just what he is. What he does. How he gets that way."

Wagner picked up a pen from the desk and started doodling with it on a scratch pad. "I've known him on and off for years. He's an importer in a big way. I guess he's a millionaire. I wouldn't know for sure. It doesn't matter much—he's big in most of the things he does."

"And what does he do," I asked. "Outside of importing this and that from Cuba?"

He shot a quick glance at me. "So you do have some sort of information on him?"

"Not much. The guy who pushed me away from that knife-artist at the railroad station was named Jackson. He works for Weiler, or so he claims."

"I know Jackson," said Wagner at once. "He's a shadow for the big guy. He does a lot of off-the-cuff work for J. B. and I guess he's the number one lieutenant. Why you asking, Larry? What do you have to do with J. B. Weiler?"

"Nothing at all," I told him. "But it looks like he wants to hire me."

"And you're not playing along?"

"I told you I'm taking a vacation."

"You're wise," said Wagner, nodding.

But something about his expression made me ask, "What's the angle on Weiler?"

He looked at me, then smiled faintly and said, "Keen, huh? Well—Weiler has his irons in a whole lot of fires in the West Indies. About a year ago one of those fires nearly burnt his fingers. An associate of Weiler's was arrested and eventually shipped back to the States. If Weiler hadn't had such a good pull with the Commissioner he might have had a lot of awkward questions to ask—and publicly, too."

I nodded. "I figured it must have been something like that. What kind of fire was it that nearly burnt up the big guy?"

"I believe," said Wagner, staring at the wall blankly, "it was a case of suspected dope-pushing."

"Narcotics, huh?"

"That's what I said."

There was silence for a long moment, then I said, "Thanks, Wagner. See you around."

"Drop me a postal card," he called after me. I closed the door, went down the bare, echoing corridor, took the elevator to street level.

It was running on toward midnight and Manhattan's pulse was beating like a well-made Swiss watch.

2

Snowman minus monkey

I stopped by at Carl's Bar and had myself a club sandwich with my drink. I was about through when Carl moved down to the end of the bar where I sat.

"How was it, Mr. Kent?"

"Okay," I told him. I pushed the plate away. "I'll have another Scotch just to clinch it."

"Sure." He made no move to take my glass. "Mr. Kent you got any friends wear yellow ties and with dark blue shirts?"

"Not anymore," I told him. "I'm one of those old-fashioned guys."

Carl said, "There's a gent wearing the brightest yellow tie you ever did see and a shirt so deep blue it's almost black. He's sitting at a table over by the wall waiting for you to come in."

I didn't look round. "You know him?"

Carl shook his head. "He's never been in here before. I'd have found some excuse to bounce him right out again, only I figured you might just know him and might get sore."

"At you? Be your age."

"He says he heard you came to this bar a lot. Said he wanted to meet you and it was very important."

I said, "What do I owe you, Carl?"

"Leaving so soon?"

I got off the stool, glanced casually around. The little guy in the dark suit stood out like a sore boil among the more sedate drinkers. I didn't think I knew him but there was something vaguely familiar about his mug.

I said, "On second thoughts have Nicky bring me a drink over to that table by the wall."

"Sure, Mr. Kent. And one for the gent with the sporty tie?"

"Later," I told him.

I moved over to the table by the wall. The little guy was building a framework of spent matchsticks and scowling over his task. I said, "You the guy been asking about me?"

He glanced up quickly and his hand knocked over the pile of matches. He started to get to his feet.

I said, "Relax." I sat down opposite him.

"Look, Kent—"

"Mister to you."

He swallowed. He had a big Adam's apple and he overworked it. "Mr. Kent, I wanted to talk with you. I called you at your office and your apartment but I couldn't raise you—"

"That's funny," I said. "Maybe I wasn't there when you called, huh?"

Nick was there with a drink. I took it. The little guy had an empty glass in front of him with a straw broken over the lip.

I said, "Okay, what made you spend the nickels so recklessly?"

"I want to talk with you."

"Go right ahead. Won't even cost you a dime."

He had a round face, with small bright shoe-button eyes and his black hair was parted dead center and slicked down either side of his white forehead. His ears stuck out, and he had a small birth-mark on the angle of his jaw.

He said, "I'm Gus Elsinore."

And then I remembered.

He said, "Maybe you know about me, huh?"

I lowered my glass.

"Indicted 1951 by a Federal Court. Charge—dope-pushing."

"Sentence—six years," said Elsinore sulkily. "I sweated it right out, too. Only the second rap I got in my life and I didn't get one day off my calendar. I behaved myself, too."

"Too bad," I said. I took some more of my drink. "When did you hit town, Elsinore?"

"Oh, I've been around quite a while."

"You used to operate in Chicago, huh?"

"That's right," said Elsinore. As he spoke he glanced swiftly about the bar room. It was almost an instinctive movement of his eyes; the predatory animal checking for danger signals and scents and sounds; just checking.

I said, "If you're looking for a handout—"

"No," said Elsinore. Again he swallowed and I watched his Adam's apple go up and down. "I guess you wouldn't pass up a drink?"

"I'm not in the mood," I told him. I finished my own drink and started to push back from the table, but he reached out a small, quick hand and grabbed me by the wrist.

"Listen to me, will yuh?"

I glanced down at his hand and then at him. "You're nervous, son," I told him. "Go cool off some place." I was standing up.

He scrambled up after me. He said urgently, "I got somethin' to tell yuh ... about Dan Harbin—"

I said, "Looks like it's my busy night." I glanced at the watch on my wrist. "You know the Balaclava skating rink?"

He thought for a moment, then nodded vigorously.

"I'll be in the gangway, front entrance, ten minutes. Meet me there."

He ducked his head, turned and was gone, scuttling out like a scared rabbit.

I strolled over to the bar and paid my check, and Carl said evenly, "Was he worth the trouble, Mr. Kent?"

"He could be and again he could be just another good reason why I should start taking my vacation as of now." I nodded to him. "See you around, Carl."

The crowd was big at the Balaclava. There was an elimination contest under way and sections of the crowd were yelling plenty for their favorites.

I leaned against the rail halfway down the gangway. Gus Elsinore didn't interest me any more than did the doll on skates cutting a figure-eight out there. He had a record as a dope-pusher; and all along I figured dope was back of Jim Calloway's killing. Elsinore had clinched it by spilling Dan Harbin's name.

I would have been better off in bed, but I had paid my admission and there I was.

A hand touched my arm, I looked down and there he was, too, black hair shining, shoe-button eyes glittering.

"I guess we can talk here."

I said, "Start."

"You don't want to get the wrong idea about me, Kent. I don't want nothin' for myself. Just want to do you a good turn, see?"

"Okay, start doing it."

"They're going to try and get you, Kent."

Applause was breaking out as the skater finished her routine and took a bow from the center of the rink.

I said, "Harbin's pals?"

Elsinore nodded briefly. "Who else? One of the boys nearly got you tonight, didn't he?"

I leaned against the rail and looked at him.

He said uneasily, "You don't have to look at me, mister. I was around when Johnny Omar came in." He paused and I knew he was waiting for some question from me, but I said nothing.

He went on, "I was at the Excelsior Club, see? A lot of the boys were there. Johnny Omar came in and told them how he tailed you down from Ossining. He tried to get you in the crowd but somebody pushed you to one side at the last minute and Johnny missed." Elsinore shrugged. "The boys wasn't too happy over that—not over Johnny missing you but on account of they got it down the grapevine that you saw Dan Harbin before he went to the hot spot, and that Danny talked." He paused again. His eyes were bright like a bird's. "They still want to get even with you, Kent, but they're nervous about what Danny told you, so I guess they'll keep you alive long enough to make you spill."

"It takes all kinds."

"Yeah," said Elsinore. "It ain't every day of the week a guy gets condemned to death and then gets a reprieve."

"So I'm reprieved, huh?"

"I'm givin' it to you straight, mister. They're out to get you, but they sure want to know what Dan Harbin spilled to you before they put you in the East River."

"*You* start spilling, Elsinore. Who's 'they'?"

He shook his head. "Just a bunch of guys."

I glanced around. A few people were standing in the alley in front of us, and all were intent on the show out front. I grabbed Elsinore's wrist, rammed him hard against the tiled wall. I saw his eyes starting with fear.

"Okay, let's have it. Why did you contact me?"

His lips scarcely moved. "I—I had to get even."

"Who with?"

"Gondola."

"Is he carrying the torch for Danny Harbin?"

"I guess so."

"Why do you want to get even?"

"He loused up a deal. He double-crossed me too many times over deals."

"Dope?"

"I guess you could call it that. Say, Kent, you're breaking my arm—"

"Why the big squeal, Elsinore? Come on, let's have it."

"I told you." He squirmed in my grasp. "I just had to get a needle into Gondola. When I heard them talking about you, I figured it was as good a way as any. Look, Kent, say we make a deal, huh?"

"Keep talking."

"I'll spill anything you want to know, only—get me alongside Albanesi."

"Who's he?"

At once I saw the shutters fall over his eyes. His face smoothed into a mask.

I said, "Okay, if that's the way you want it, Elsinore—" I leaned on his wrist.

He uttered a yelp. I saw a guy down the gangway turn his head casually. I leaned right over Elsinore. I said close to his ear, "If it isn't now, it'll be some other time. Who's Albanesi?" I let him go and stepped back. I took out a cigarette and made a play of lighting it.

Elsinore leaned against the wall, massaging his wrist, swearing to himself. When he was through I said, "Okay, what's it to be?"

He said sulkily, "I figured we'd get along fine. Maybe I had you wrong."

"About Albanesi?"

"Could be."

"Who is he, Elsinore?"

"A guy down in Cuba."

Cuba! The bells were ringing. ...

"Oh, yeah," I said casually. "That guy." Then I made a shot in the dark. "I guess Johnny Omar, the knife-artist, recognized Jackson back there at the railroad terminal?"

I saw Elsinore nod. He was still scowling, but for me the pieces in the jigsaw were falling into place. I dragged on my cigarette. I said, "Okay, so I get alongside Albanesi. What's in it for you?"

"A whole lot," he said eagerly. "All I want you to do is give me a break with Albanesi. What you say, Kent? Will you play along?"

"It could be some time before I contact Albanesi," I said, making it sound like I was worried. "I'm taking off on a vacation tomorrow."

Elsinore blurted out, "Vacation! You mean you're quittin' town on account of Gondola and the boys?"

"I didn't say why I was quitting town."

As if a light had broken on him he said, "Oh, sure, I get it. You're headin' down to Havana! Well—I'll be going there myself in the next few days. If you want to do the right thing by me, Kent, you call me at the Esperance Hotel, just off the Prado. Remember that, huh?"

"Sure," I said. "Why not? It's an easy name to remember."

He nodded. Again his eyes roamed around. "You do the right thing by me, Kent, and I'll sure give you plenty in return. I'm a guy like that. Big-hearted."

"Great," I told him. "Go buy fire-insurance."

He stared at me.

"Gondola's a mobster. He's also lucky he didn't follow Danny Harbin to the chair—I guess he would have only the cops had nothing on him. How you figure he's going to feel when he finds out you've been squealing?"

Elsinore laughed, an unpleasant sound. "You goin' to put the finger on me, Kent?"

"Did I say that?"

He shrugged. "I trust you, you trust me. And—thanks for the advice, only that punk Gondola will have to get up early in the morning to catch me." He started to move away. I grabbed him by the arm and swung him round.

"Where you staying in town?"

"It doesn't matter—"

"It does to me."

"I'm at the Columbus Hotel on Lower 14th. I'll be there, maybe a coupla days. Say, Kent?"

"Uh-huh?"

"Don't get any funny ideas about puttin' the cops onto me. That wouldn't be smart, now would it?"

"You tell me why it wouldn't?"

He said carefully, "The way I'm fixed I can see the ball bouncing both ways. I know what Gondola's got in mind, and I know what you're doin', too, and I figure I can make that ball bounce just whichever way I want it to. You with me, Kent?"

I said, "Get out of my hair, louse."

I stood watching him as he swaggered away, his yellow tie gleaming like a beacon. He walked like a guy who had plenty on his mind, a lot of ideas on where he was going and what he was going to do.

The way things were shaping I hoped Gondola didn't get him—not right away.

***

I went up town, checked at my office for late mail, then took a taxi round to my apartment block. I paid off the cab and was crossing the sidewalk toward the entrance when I saw a car slide to a stop at the curb.

I had a brief glimpse of a dame getting out like she was in a hurry. Then I moved on into the lobby. I was at the elevator when I heard a sound behind me. I turned and there she was—the dame who had got out of the car, tall, sleek, very dark. She was smiling.

"You're in an awful hurry, Mr. Kent."

"I usually am."

"You don't know me?"

"I guess I will."

"I'm Lolita."

"Lolita what?"

"Albanesi."

I guess I didn't let my thoughts show.

The elevator was on automatic. I pulled the door back and waited.

"After you," said the dame.

"You going someplace?"

"Of course," she said. "I'm coming up to see you. I followed you all the way over from your office building."

"F.B.I., maybe?"

She laughed, showing very white teeth, then hipped her way into the elevator and waited while I let the doors close smoothly and thumbed the buzzer to take us up.

She didn't say anything until the elevator stopped at my floor. Then she turned her head and smiled at me and said, "I guess you weren't expecting me?"

"If I'd known you were coming I'd have broken out flags."

"Wonderful!" She stepped out the elevator and I followed her down the hall.

As I juggled the key to the lock she said, "I know all about you but you don't know anything about me, do you?"

I said nothing, pushed the door open for her to enter. She made no move for a moment, stood there looking at me, her head a little on one side. She was wearing a sort of high-collared evening cape over her ballerina dress. She had a lot of that chunky jewelry some dames wear—and on Lolita it looked dead right.

"You know," she said, "you should have heard of me. After all you did a lot of investigation into the Calloway murder, didn't you?"

"Inside," I told her.

She shrugged a shapely shoulder and moved into the apartment. As I closed the door I heard her cry, "Why, this is far too comfortable for a bachelor!"

"Yeah," I said. "One of Manhattan's showplaces. What'll it be? Scotch, bourbon, rye—"

"Don't you have anything but whisky?"

"Sure," I said. "That's the bar over there. Go help yourself."

She pouted. "That's hardly a way to treat a lady, and a guest what's more."

"Uninvited," I pointed out.

She went to the davenport, sat on it with determination and skillfully crossed her legs. When I tore my eyes back to her face, I saw she was still pouting.

I said, "Where are your buddies?"

The scowl vanished. She looked at me in surprise. "Buddies?" she echoed.

"Yeah," I said. "The guys you left back there in the auto."

"Oh." She gave a little laugh. An uneasy laugh. "I came alone, actually."

"The hell you did. You weren't driving that auto, baby."

"It's a rented one. I have a paid chauffeur."

"Living it up, huh?"

She said nothing.

I moved over to the bar, poured myself a Scotch.

Lolita said plaintively, "Could I have a gin, please? A large one?"

"What with it?"

"Oh, just anything. More gin, maybe." She laughed.

"Quite a party girl," I told her.

I carried a glass over to her. As I put it into her hand she imprisoned my fingers. We looked at each other for a long moment, then she said, "You don't have to be suspicious of me, Larry. I'm quite a harmless person, really."

"Yeah," I said. "It shows, too."

She released my hand and sank back with a laugh. "Now I feel there's a compliment back of that." She patted the cushion beside her. "Won't you sit down?"

"Sure," I said. "Later." I moved over to a chair and sat on the arm of it, drank some of my whisky, watching her.

She stared at the glass in her hand and said, "You were at the prison today, weren't you, when Danny Harbin was executed?"

I said nothing.

She glanced up at me seriously. "I'm not going to be inquisitive. It's just that certain people I know were interested in Danny Harbin and—because of all the work you did—in you." She spoke smoothly, but with a hint of foreign accent which came out now and then; it helped to make her voice cute. I wondered which team she played on—Gondola's or J. B. Weiler's. I wasn't kept long in doubt.

She moved restlessly on the davenport and said suddenly, "Could I have a cigarette?"

I shook one from the package and held it out to her.

She parted her lips and I placed the cigarette between them. She stayed that way, her eyes half-closed while I held the lighter to the cigarette. She sank back again, letting the smoke trickle.

"Jackson told me you were playing very hard to get. It struck me as a good idea to come along and try my feminine wiles on you."

"Say, that's quite an idea." I finished off my drink, walked over to the bar and poured a fresh one. Turning to look at her I added, "There's one thing about you, baby. You're about as subtle as a jack-hammer."

I heard her laugh, then she said, "I would be insulting you if I tried to pretend to be something I wasn't. I rate your intelligence high, you see."

I went over to the davenport and leaned over her. "Okay," I said. "So you're playing along with Jackson?"

"Of course," she nodded. She took a sip of her drink. Her eyes were big, black, the pupils large. She had a habit of staring fixedly; almost like she was trying to mesmerize a guy. She needn't have bothered; the way she was stacked no guy would stand a chance within ten feet of Lolita.

She said, "I'm from Cuba. My father is down there. He has a lot of interests that run parallel to J. B. Weiler's. They have a lot of dealings together."

"Uh-huh?"

"So you see I have quite an interest in J. B. Weiler's affairs."

"You do, huh?"

She half-smiled at me. "I'll get to the point right away, Larry. Tonight Jackson told me he'd approached you on behalf of J. B. and tried to persuade you into taking a case for the old man. He told me about all the trouble you'd had at the terminal and—well, it seemed to me it might be a smart thing if you took that vacation of yours down Cuba way." She reached up a white hand and grabbed my arm. "Come closer, Larry, I'm getting a wacky neck looking up at you."

I wound up alongside her on the davenport. She slid her arm around my neck. The way she held me I figured a boa constrictor wouldn't have had a show against Lolita, either.

"Keep talking, baby," I told her.

She said, "It's very important to me that somebody goes down to Havana for J. B. Weiler. I'd like it to be you."

"Doing what for J. B. Weiler?"

"I think he'd better tell you that himself."

"What goes on around here? You figure you can sweet-talk me into doing something with a guy I don't even know? Jackson fell down on it, and—baby, you're headed that way, too."

"I wouldn't bet on it, Larry," she said softly. She was still half smiling and her eyes were hooded by eyelashes, long, black and curling.

I said, "I'm not a betting man."

"All you have to do is call him up tomorrow morning. Go have a talk with him."

"And the pay-off?"

She hesitated and then, "I believe Jackson offered you five hundred dollars. I'm sure J. B. will go higher than that. With all expenses paid, of course."

"Big deal, huh?"

"It's very important."

"And," I said, "where does Gondola fit in?"

"Gondola?" She looked shocked.

"Just another guy. Say—finish your drink."

"I don't want any more." She held out her glass with her free hand.

I took it from her, broke her grip and put her glass and mine on the small table by the davenport. Then she was grabbing at me again.

I said, "Business first, baby."

"Why not—later, Larry?" Then I felt her mouth against mine, hard and eager. It wasn't a kiss, it was an explosion.

***

"Now, Larry?"

"Take it easy," I told her. I finished the drink I had just poured and put the glass back on the bar-top. Then I moved over to the telephone. She repeated the number for me. As I dialed I glanced over to where she lay back on the cushions of the davenport, like a sleepy cat, long, lithe, dark ... I wrenched my attention back to the phone. A guy had replied in the smooth tones of a well-trained houseboy.

"Give me J. B. Weiler."

"I'm sorry, sir, he's not to be disturbed."

"Tell him it's Larry Kent."

"One moment, sir. I'll tell him." He went away and I glanced again at Lolita, who flipped a hand at me and blew a kiss. I said, "Fix me a cigarette, baby."

"Of course, Larry." She wriggled off the davenport in one sinuous movement. She got my cigarettes from the side table, lit one and put it between my lips. Then she bit me on the ear just as the guy from Weiler's house came on the wire.

"Mr. Kent, Mr. Weiler's coming on now."

"Okay."

Lolita was smiling at me. As I slipped my hand over the speaker she said, "I knew you'd see it my way, Larry."

"Yeah," I said. I didn't tell her that I'd already figured that the smart thing to do was contact Weiler and see what steamed back of that big guy who had interests in Havana, Cuba—who had a hireling walked around in a shabby Panama hat—and a business contact with a daughter the spectacular shape of Lolita Albanesi.

"Hello!" There was a bellow down the line and I held the receiver a half-inch from my ear as I replied.

"This is Kent. That you, Weiler?"

"This is J. B. Weiler. I want to see you, young man."

"Okay," I said. "Make a date."

"Right away."

"No dice. It's too late."

"It's never too late for me," he roared back. "I'll expect you inside an hour."

I shrugged, dropped the receiver back on its cradle. As I turned to face Lolita, she said, "I could hear him. His bark's definitely as bad as his bite."

I went over to the bar and had myself another drink.

"Maybe I could drop you off some place?" I asked her as I pulled on a light coat over my suit.

"It doesn't matter. The auto will be waiting for me."

"Patient guy, huh?"

"Of course," said Lolita. "But you're not going right away, are you, Larry?"

"You heard what the man said."

"But—" She was pouting. "I thought we could—well —talk some more—"

"Later," I told her. I slapped her seat as she went out the door. She swayed in front of me all the way down to the elevator, patting her dark hair. Her perfume filled the elevator car as we rode down—and it stayed with me all the way across town in a taxi, where I went to keep the date with J. B. Weiler.

***

There was no sign of Jackson at the penthouse apartment where I was admitted by a short, smooth-faced guy wearing a black silk jacket and the whitest shirt I'd ever seen.

"Mr. Weiler's expecting you, sir."

"Uh-huh."

"Come this way." He led me into a room, waved to a chair. "Mr. Weiler won't be a moment."

I didn't sit down. I looked around the room, then lit a cigarette. Behind me the door closed sharply and I turned to see a tall, craggy old guy with a clipped white moustache over a rat-trap mouth, fierce blue eyes beneath jutting white eyebrows.

"So you got here at last?"

"Looks like it."

"Don't scatter ash over my carpet. You'll find trays around the room."

I stared at him.

"Sit down, won't you?"

"I'm okay."

He stood and eyed me for a long moment and then, "Well, I've certainly heard a lot about you, Kent. The latest bulletin has it that you're not too happy about taking on a new assignment right now."

"I've changed my mind," I told him.

He stroked his grizzled moustache and gave a faint smile. "Lolita's a very persuasive lady, don't you think?"

"Yeah."

"She told Jackson she'd get you, and—here you are."

He went over to a small table by the wall, sat back of it, slid out a drawer and as he produced a slim manila file, said, "I'm very glad you showed up. I put two other men on this job and both of them fell down on it. I reached the stage where I was starting to think I'd have to put pressure on the law to help me and that I didn't want." He shot me a quick look from under his shaggy eyebrows.

I shrugged and mashed out my cigarette. "One of those assignments, huh?"

"Don't get me wrong," said Weiler. "And I wish you'd sit down."

"Okay." I took a chair close to the desk-table.

He laid his big hands on the manila folder and said, "In the first place I take it you know who I am, what my interests are in Cuba?"

"Some."

"I have a representative down there. He supervises all my agency business from Havana. His name is Rock Alison. Something's happened to him, and I want that you go and find him."

"That all?"

"All?" He laid his hands on the table, hitched himself forward and glared at me. "I understand you had more imagination than to say a thing like that. These days Havana is a city of unrest. Business has been very confused the last few months and I can assure you that none of us are any too happy about the state of affairs down there. Now—it seems Rock Alison has run into some kind of trouble and he can't be located. It'll be by no means easy to find him and bring him home."

"On account of this political trouble?"

"Not only that," replied Weiler. "I believe there's been a conspiracy operating against Alison. You see, at the time of his disappearance a whole lot of my money disappeared with him."

"Uh-huh?"

"Something like fifty-thousand dollars. To me, the loss isn't shattering, but it's still a lot of money."

"In any language," I said.

"Exactly. Quite obviously the inference would be that Alison had absconded with my Havana reserves to the tune of fifty-thousand dollars. But I know Alison better than that. At least I think I do."

"You figure he wouldn't pull that, huh?"

"I wouldn't go so far as to say that. I guess most men get tempted at some time or other in their lives. And as I said before, it is a large amount of money. But—"

"You got other reasons?"

"Yes. Alison sent me a report just two days before he disappeared. I'll show you that report presently. That is, if you're prepared to take on the assignment."

"Keep talking," I told him.

"In this report he mentions something that had been troubling him for some time—certain shipments of his had been interfered with and he had run into trouble, not only on the waterfront but among shipping-agents as well." He glared at me. "I want you to understand that Alison is a very level-headed young man."

"Young, huh?"

"He wouldn't be any older than you. He has a good head on his shoulders, and he's not the kind of man to be bluffed by a pack of mountebanks. They're not political mountebanks, either. I want that clearly understood. It's none of my business how the Cubans run their country. I'm a businessman, Kent. First, last and all the time. Well, now, where was I?"

I took out another cigarette, stifling the yawn. It had been a long, hard night. I said, "This report makes it unlikely Alison was thinking about absconding with your money?"

"Exactly," said Weiler. "It's my firm belief that he's run into trouble with these same people who have been making life difficult for him these last few months. Naturally, when he didn't contact me after forty-eight hours, I called the Cuban police long-distance. They promised a routine investigation, but I had a reply from them only this afternoon. It was quite a negative report, and it's obvious to me they're not taking their work seriously."

"How about the American Consul down there?"

"I didn't try him."

"For the same reason that you don't want the U.S. law to help you find Alison?"

He shot a quick look at me and then smiled, showing his big teeth. "You're very astute, Mr. Kent. Yes, that is precisely the reason. The truth of the matter is, the last thing I want at this moment is a top-level police investigation into Alison's dealings with certain people."

"Albanesi, maybe?"

"You're guessing, Mr. Kent." Again he smiled, then went on. "Right through, Alison believed that racketeers were making use of our merchandising service to smuggle dope into the U.S. from Havana."

"Dope, huh?"

"Heroin mostly, and some crude opium. Well now, it's a very intricate business importing from a city like Havana. I don't suppose you'll appreciate it, but matters could become—difficult if the police started nosing around. They could quite easily come to the wrong conclusions about the activities of J. B. Weiler in Havana."

He met my eye. I said nothing for a moment and then, "I get the picture. You don't want police investigation because you're afraid you might get your name smeared. But how about the little cops you put on to find Alison?"

"I'm not worried about anything they can do." He shrugged, added, "You drink?"

"Frequently."

He reached out and pressed a bell.

The smooth house-boy moved in, smooth as silk.

"Fetch some drinks."

The house-boy disappeared and Weiler said to me, "Get the picture clearly in your mind. I'm no dope-runner. I make enough money as it is, without asking for trouble handling illicit dope."

"I guessed so," I told him. "That was one close shave you had with the cops down there a while back."

He reddened slightly. He snapped, "You been probing into my affairs?"

"I don't have to probe," I told him. "Some things stick right out for anybody to see."

"You won't be seeing anything that reflects badly on my name," said the old man. He hoisted himself out of the chair, strode round the side of the desk, looked down at me.

"Listen to me." I leaned back in my seat and he said, "I'm a rich man, Kent, and I've got a lot of power both here and in Havana. Rock Alison is most valuable to me and I want him found. Never mind the rest of it—my reluctance to let the F.B.I. in on an investigation—the point is, will you take the assignment?"

"Do I have to tell you now?"

"Why leave it until tomorrow?" He turned as the houseboy came into the room bearing a tray laden with drinks. "Put it on the table, Henry."

Henry nodded and after asking me what I wanted poured me a drink. J. B. had himself a white rum, I noticed. He didn't break it down with water, either.

As Henry left the room, Weiler said, "Here's to your health?

"You figure I might need extra insurance if I go down to Havana?

I'm vaccinated. Even against Havana fever."

"I'm glad to hear that." He paused with the glass halfway to his lips. "I take it you're not a nervous man?"

"I'm too tired," I told him, "to be nervous." I drained my glass, dropped it back on the tray.

Weiler rolled the rum around his mouth before swallowing it, then he rumbled, "I'll pay you well to go to Havana and find Alison. Five hundred dollars if you locate him and five hundred if you send him back to me safe and sound. Is it a deal?"

"With first-class expenses," I pointed out.

"Sure, sure," he said impatiently. "What's more, Mr. Kent, I can make the proposition even more attractive to you."

He paused and I said, "Bonus, maybe?"

"I understand you were a great friend of James Calloway, the man who was murdered by Dan Harbin."

"What of it?" I guess my tone was steely.

Weiler said, "It's ancient history now. Your friend's dead and Harbin's electrocuted. Only—the way I heard it you might still be interested in tying up the case to your satisfaction."

"What are you getting at, Weiler?"

"Just this," said J.B. He planted his big fists on the tabletop and leaned on them. "If you go to Havana you might find the dope ring operating down there has some connection with the one-time mobster, Dan Harbin. Your investigations could get you some place, Kent. That is—if you're smart and receptive to new ideas."

"Skip the sales talk. You've sold me. I'll take a check now, Weiler."

He fingered his moustache, his eyes wary. "You're very direct, aren't you?"

"Yeah."

"Well, sit down and have yourself another drink, while I write you a check, and then I'll have you run through these papers, including the last report Rock Alison mailed me from Havana." He picked up the manila folder. "Is it a deal, Kent?"

"Sure," I said. "I could use some of that Cuban togetherness. How soon do the planes fly out?"

3

Blondes do it all the time

Next morning I tried to contact Benjie Sorensen at the Narcotics Bureau, Washington. No dice. Sorensen was out of town. I hung up, wrote him at some length, went out and marked the letter air-express. I went back to the office, thoughtfully.

Back at my desk, it was so quiet I could hear my stomach rumbling. I scratched my chin thoughtfully and watched a fly crawling through a patch of sunlight on my desk top. Benjie Sorensen had been a good friend of Jim Calloway's in the old days, and it was largely through him that Calloway got the job in the Narcotics Bureau after the war. That report on the Calloway killing in the *Clarion* had been wrong on one point: Jim Calloway *had* been engaged in outside operative work, but not in recent years. It happened not long after he joined the Federal Service. But he didn't last long at it. An old war-wound forced him to take a desk job in the Bureau, and there he stayed until the time of his death.

The fly was rubbing its paws over its head in the sunlight. The telephone started ringing.

It was J. B. Weiler.

"I've arranged the flight for you," he barked, without preamble. "Take-off's at twelve. I'm sending Jackson around with the flight ticket."

"Okay," I said. "That all?"

"What more do you want?" The old man sounded peevish. "You'll stay at the Hotel of the Americas in Havana, and you'll call me each night and give me a verbal report. And the moment you get any definite news of Alison, send me a radio telegram."

I said, "Spare me expenses, huh?"

"You're being paid," he snarled.

"By the way, Weiler, you know a man named Elsinore? Gus Elsinore?"

There was a silence down the wire for a moment and then, "I never heard of him before in my life."

"Okay," I said. "See you when I get back."

"Make it a fast job," he snapped. "I want results!"

I heard the click at the other end as he hung up.

Slowly I replaced the phone on its cradle. I opened the top drawer and took out an unbroken package of cigarettes. As I unsealed it the phone rang again. I tossed the cigarette package on the desk, and the sun-baking fly quit.

"Hello, Larry."

Lolita.

"How are you feeling today, honey?"

"Never better," I told her.

"A little bird told me that you're flying down to Cuba very soon."

"Sure."

I heard her laugh. A rich, gurgling sound, and instantly I had a picture of her as she had been the night before... .

I deliberately switched my mind back to the present. "You figuring on going back to Cuba?"

"Oh, yes, Larry. All my interests are there, you know—especially now I know you'll be in Havana. Do you tango?"

"I didn't think anybody did any more."

"Oh, but, Larry, you'd be surprised!"

"I bet I would. Any big reason for calling me, honey?"

"Isn't it enough that I just want to tell you hello?"

I could almost see her pouting at the other end. She went on quickly, "Larry, there's just one thing."

"Yeah?"

"Be careful, won't you?"

"What of? Latin-American dames?"

I heard her laughing again. "You think I'm nice, Larry?"

"Cute as bugs' ears."

"I'm glad."

A small noise came down the wire and she said, "That was me sending you a kiss."

"Great," I told her. "See you around, Lolita." I hung up, reached for the cigarettes and lit one.

There came a knock on the door. It looked like being my busy day.

"Come in. The lock's off."

The door opened and there stood Jackson. "Good morning, Mr. Kent."

I grunted.

He came in, taking off his Panama hat. I saw he was bald. Without that Panama he had a mournful look, like a missionary who'd just heard that a native chief had ordered garlic that day.

Jackson took a folder from his pocket and dropped it on the desk before me. "Your flight tickets, Mr. Kent."

"Yeah, Weiler phoned me about them." I put the folder in my pocket and Jackson said, "I'm so glad you're taking on this case, Mr. Kent."

"Yeah?"

"I must admit I didn't think you would do it, but Lolita was very confident. She usually gets what she wants."

I leaned back in my chair and let the smoke trickle. I said, "Sit down if it'll make you feel better."

"Thank you, Mr. Kent." He carefully picked up a chair and carried it over to the desk and sat on it, and folded his hands over that battered Panama.

I said, "What gives with Lolita Albanesi?"

His eyebrows went up. "I don't know what you mean, Mr. Kent."

"Where does she fit into the Weiler organization?"

"Oh, that's easily explained. Her father does a lot of business with J. B. in Cuba. And Lolita was always friendly with J. B.'s daughter."

"Daughter?" I guess I sounded surprised.

Jackson nodded smugly. "J. B. was married once. Carol is his only child. She's a beautiful girl, Mr. Kent, and—before I forget, she asked me if you'd meet her this morning."

I stared at him. "Meet Carol Weiler? What gives?"

"It so happens," said Jackson carefully, "that Miss Weiler is flying down to Havana, too, and J. B. thought it might be a good idea if she went along with you. You could be company for each other and—"

"Now, wait a minute," I broke in. "How old is this doll I'm supposed to nursemaid?"

"About twenty-one or twenty-two, I suppose."

"And I suppose you figure this dame's going along just for thrills?"

"Oh, no, Mr. Kent," he said leaning forward earnestly, "Nothing like that. Carol is a very capable and independent young lady. She's spent a lot of time in Havana—that's where she met Lolita of course, and she takes a keen interest in her father's business affairs."

I said, "This case is starting to stink."

"But, Mr. Kent—I had no idea you had any prejudice against young ladies?"

I looked at him. I said nothing.

Jackson went on, "I'm sure Miss Weiler will be no liability. Her father has asked her expressly to go down with you to Havana, just in case you need help. After all, she knows a great many people down there, and she could make your work a lot easier."

"I get it. Carol goes along as her old man's stooge—to check on me."

"No, it isn't like that at all—"

I cut in, "Okay, okay, skip it. Where do I meet this dame?"

"She's having coffee at a place called the Pincushion on Madison Avenue—"

I got up, mashed out my cigarette. "Pincushion, huh? So she's one of those dames—rich man's daughter pretends to take a great interest in his affairs—spends her time drinking coffee in some jade-green joint called the Pincushion, where the long-hairs gather and talk about hi-fi and sex. Okay, Jackson, it looks like my working vacation has started."

He got up. He was smiling nervously. "I sure hope everything works out all right."

"It will," I assured him. "I'll fly down to Havana with this cute millionaire's daughter and when I get there I'll probably find Rock Alison's been fished out of the harbor and the case is closed. You know something, Jackson? I should have packed my fishing pole and flown out to Maine last night."

I picked up the phone and called the janitor of my apartment block, checked to see if he had my luggage okay.

"Have it round at the airport at eleven-thirty," I told him. "I'm flying out at twelve."

"Okay, Mr. Kent. I'll fix everything."

I hung up.

Jackson was still standing there patiently, his Panama clutched in his hand.

I said, "You did quite a job saving my neck last night. You know who that guy was with the knife?"

He blinked.

"He was a guy name of Johnny Omar. That name mean anything to you?"

He shook his head mutely.

"Jackson, I bet you never heard of Gus Elsinore either?" He blinked again.

"No talk, huh?"

"I don't know what you're getting at, Mr. Kent. About that man with the knife—"

"Forget him." I checked the locker that contained a few private papers I carried, and my spare bottle of Scotch. "Okay," I said. "Let's go."

We went out. The Sun was shining, but right then I wasn't caring. It could have been blowing a hurricane and I wouldn't even have raised my eyebrows. I was tired.

I took a cab and dropped Jackson off down the block. I paid off the cab on Madison Avenue, following Jackson's directions.

The Pincushion was crammed between tall buildings, a self-effacing joint. It was a tiny place with a front door at the bottom of a half-dozen steps. The sign outside was discreet and so was the lighting inside. As I went in, it was as if I had walked out of sunshine into the middle of the night. There were soft fluorescents in the ceiling, and around the walls discreetly-shaded little lamps. Cute. I could almost smell the espresso coffee and I looked around for dames with pony-tails and guys with hair growing over their ears. Then I saw the bar. It was at the far end of the long, narrow room, and a white-jacketed bartender worked under a strong light. There were a couple of people on stools at the bar.

At an angle to it stood a counter and sure enough there was an espresso machine steaming away, doubtless making a fortune for its owner. The joint was surprisingly full for that time of day, and there was a low murmur of talk.

I walked right through to the liquor bar, and the guy in the white jacket glanced up.

"Yes, sir?" he asked politely.

"Scotch on the rocks."

"Any particular brand, sir?"

I looked at him. "Can a guy nominate it?"

"Why not?" His tone was still polite, his eyes shrewdly on me.

I named my favorite brand and the bartender reached for a bottle. He made magic with a glass, crushed ice—and the Scotch.

I squeezed onto one of the leather-topped stools. As I dropped a bill on the bar top, I said, "Quite a place you got here."

"One of the best in this part of town," said the bartender chattily. "You've just discovered the place, sir?"

"Yeah," I said. "I'm slumming." I took some of my drink. I was starting to feel better.

A voice from behind me said, "Are you going to drink all the way to Havana?"

I didn't turn around right away. I was inhaling the scent of her and it was powerful, yet elusive; a mixture of jasmine and something else I couldn't put my taste-buds to.

The bartender said, "Good morning, Miss Weiler," and the dame rustled quickly past me and took the stool alongside.

I looked at her then.

It was a day full of surprises.

She was a honey-blonde with darker eyebrows, and the kind of blue eyes a guy can go crazy over. If he's that kind of guy. For the rest—I had an impression of a wide, curving red mouth, a stubborn little chin, and a throat that swept tantalizing down to a froth of nylon shirt. She was wearing one of those tailored suits that carry a London tag, or the name of a Rome maker, or the flavor of the Rue de la Paix.

"I'm Carol Weiler."

"Sure," I said. "What are you drinking?"

"Coffee."

I shrugged.

The bartender said, "Another Scotch?"

"Skip it," I told him. I got off the stool.

Carol Weiler looked up at me.

I said, "There's a vacant table back there."

"If you like." Her tone was cool, her eyes unfriendly.

We moved over to the table beneath one of the red shaded lamps. A waiter came and I ordered coffee and club sandwiches for two. When the waiter had gone again, Carol Weiler stripped off her gloves and said, "I thought it would be a good idea to meet you before we actually flew out."

"Uh-huh."

"I saw you last night when you were leaving my father's penthouse, and it was after that I decided to go down to Havana, too."

"Uh-huh?"

"I just paid you a big compliment."

I looked at her. "What's the real reason for wanting to go to Havana?"

She matched my stare. "It so happens that I'm very fond of Rock Alison."

"Like that, huh?"

"Like any way you please, Mr. Kent. Now I'll trouble you not to pry further into my private affairs."

"Are you kidding? Finish your sandwich and let's get out of here. We've got a plane to catch."

I saw her flush slightly. She bent her head over her plate.

Under cover of lighting a cigarette I took another close look at her.

That dame certainly had just about everything—but it looked like she was carrying a torch for a guy who was so close to being dead you could almost smell the lilies.

"Excuse me, Miss Weiler—"

Carol looked up quickly. I saw first of all surprise in her face and then a faint flush of anger.

"What do you want?" she demanded.

The guy, well-dressed in a flashy way, said, "It isn't me, miss, it's the Duke. He wants to see you."

I glanced again at Carol and saw her moisten her lips, quickly. Then, as if with an effort she said, "How did you know I was here?"

The guy said indifferently, "We checked."

Carol looked at me.

I kept my face deadpan.

She said, "If you don't mind, Mr. Kent—"

"Sure, sure, go ahead." I glanced at my wrist watch. "It's time we broke it up."

"Yeah," said the guy. "Hurry it, willya."

I saw Carol's flush deepen. She said angrily, "Where is he waiting?"

"Right outside in his car. We came around when we heard you was here."

"If you'll excuse me, Larry?"

Larry—just like that.

I got up as she moved away from the table. Over her shoulder she said, "See you at the airport, before noon."

"Sure."

The guy squinted at me and walked out after the blonde.

As soon as they were out of sight I dropped money on the table and moved quickly to the door. I glanced toward the curb and sure enough there was a big maroon-colored Cadillac parked there—where it had no right to be. Carol Weiler was standing close to it, talking vehemently with a guy inches shorter than she was. He wore a bow tie and his clothes were sharp. He had no hat on and I saw that his black hair was receding. From where I stood he seemed to be in his forties, sleek, well-preserved.

The guy who had brought Carol out of the restaurant was standing with his hand on the door, waiting.

I strolled casually down the sidewalk, keeping passers-by between me and the car. Then I moved over to the curb and took the number of the Cadillac. I had a glimpse of Carol getting into the car, the guy in the bow tie following her.

I moved quickly into the crowd, headed for a drugstore and went inside. I picked up a glossy magazine, thumbed it over, then glanced out through the glass door, but could see no sign of anybody hanging around.

I went to the telephone booth and called police headquarters. Wagner came on right away.

"I've been looking for you all over. Where in hell you been?"

"Around. What's burning, Wagner?"

"You know Johnny Omar?"

I stared at the blank wall of the telephone booth. I said, "Should I know him?"

"Your name and phone number were found on his body."

"Body, huh?"

"He was found back of a gas-station on a vacant lot near the Holland Tunnel entrance early this morning. He was beaten up before they shot him."

I remembered the guy at the railhead terminal—the open knife blade in his hand. I said, "Sounds like the guy who made a pass at me yesterday."

Wagner said, "Could be. He had a knife scabbard strapped to his wrist, but no knife. What's more to the point, he called headquarters around midnight last night. Said he wanted to do some talking. You can figure the rest for yourself."

"They got wise to the squeal?"

"Sure looks like it," said Wagner. "We've got the dragnet out. But—" he added, "it would maybe help a lot if you came across."

"With what?"

"Anything you might know. You better come down to headquarters, Kent."

When Wagner talked like that it wasn't smart to stall, but I told him that I was due to fly out for Havana on the noon plane.

"You got time," replied the cop briskly. "Make it right away."

***

I had the mug file spread over the table. I tapped my forefinger on one of the prints.

"This is the guy."

"Right," said Wagner in a satisfied tone. "Johnny Omar in person. Or should I say, the late Johnny Omar."

"No flowers. What's on your mind, Wagner?"

He looked at me for a moment in silence. "You got any idea about Omar?"

I shrugged, lit a cigarette. "I guess he's one of Gondola's bunch."

"Whitey Gondola?"

I nodded. "A guy contacted me last night—wanted to make a deal." I paused, wondering just how much I should spill to Wagner. Then I remembered that I was due to fly out to Havana inside an hour. Right then I didn't have the time to fool around—not with a guy like Wagner. I said, "I told you I was going to try and find out what lay behind the Calloway killing. Jim worked in the Narcotics Bureau and he was bumped off for no apparent reason—"

"Except a woman," said Wagner bluntly.

"Sure. Some mysterious dame who never appeared and whose name was never even mentioned. At all events, the guy who got the hot squat yesterday had friends, and those friends are tied in with dope."

"Start interesting me," said Wagner.

"Right now," I replied, "there's not all that much to interest a New York cop—except where it touches on this new killing, of Johnny Omar. But it's my hunch there's a drug ring operating from Havana, Cuba. In some way, somehow, some place, the friends of the late Danny Harbin are mixed up in that ring. My contact last night told me who the knife expert was, this Johnny Omar. He also told me that Harbin's friends were out to get me, but they wanted to get me alive so I could tell them what Harbin had spilled before he took his last walk."

Wagner said in a surprised tone, "But Harbin didn't spill anything to you!"

"Dead right. But it must have come down the grapevine, maybe through some friendly screw at the pen, that I'd had a last minute talk-fest with Harbin. They want to know how much he said, what he said, just what did happen in that death cell." I gave a short laugh. "Right now, I wouldn't disillusion them, not for worlds."

"Not even if it means going on a hot squat yourself? This Gondola's a mean one. He was a hatchet man for the mobsters ten years back—"

"Yeah," I broke in, "and that leads me to somebody else. Duke Cerise."

"What about him?"

"Has he been operating around this town lately?"

Wagner shook his head, pursing his lips. "As far as I can make out, Cerise hasn't tangled with the law in years. The Feds got him on that income-tax evasion rap four-five years back, and it looked like he was going to jail for the first time in his life. But Cerise beat that rap, too." He added keenly, "You got a special reason for checking on Cerise?"

"I never knew him. I'd like to see the mug files."

"That's easy fixed." He turned and beckoned an assistant who hurried forward. Wagner gave him a couple of instructions as I lit a fresh cigarette. We were standing in the records divisions at headquarters, and the room was filled with a silent, intense concentration.

Wagner was back with me.

"Larry, this contact of yours—"

"Yeah," I said. "A smart little operator who's broken with Gondola, or says he has. Maybe he was like the late Johnny Omar, and maybe he'll wind up the way Johnny did. Shot and beaten up and dropped in a vacant lot. The deal he made with me was to trade information about Gondola's activities, for an introduction I could give him to a big wheel in Havana."

"Such as what big wheel?"

"Guy by name of Albanesi."

Wagner rubbed his hands together. He said, "I never heard you spill so much so fast, Larry."

I glanced at the electric clock on the wall. "I'm riding that minute hand," I told him. "Also, I don't want to have you cops hauling me off that plane at the last minute. I've got a lush travelling companion, and I'd hate like hell to miss the trip."

Wagner said, "Never mind the trip. What's with this Albanesi?"

"I don't know," I told him, skating slightly over the truth. "I got the idea that he's operating in dope, and my contact wants to do private business with him."

"Nice friends you got."

"Yeah."

"These friends—they got names, huh?"

"I already gave you plenty."

Wagner laughed, not with humor. "This contact of yours, did he make you swear an oath of secrecy, maybe?"

"Nobody makes me do anything, Wagner."

"Okay, then, who is he?" Wagner's tone was blunt.

I said, "Treat him gently, Wagner."

"Why would I?"

"Because he may be useful."

"You mean—we let him run free, so he can maybe get you closer to Gondola?"

"Gondola's always close. He's as public as the Empire State. And he isn't the top guy."

"I can't promise anything, but who's your contact?"

"Gus Elsinore."

Wagner nodded thoughtfully, then beamed suddenly. "Elsinore! I remember that guy. A junky—"

"Wrong." I shook my head. "He pushes the stuff but doesn't use it."

"One of those, huh?"

"Yeah," I said. "You'll find him at the Columbus Hotel. Or maybe you won't. I wouldn't know."

Wagner was reaching for the phone.

I said, "Remember what I told you about the long rope." Wagner started talking busily into the phone. As he hung up, the police clerk came forward and laid a flat file on the table in front of him.

"Thanks, Jerry," said Wagner. He opened up the file. "This is kinda moth-eaten, Larry. We haven't had to use this file in years. Take a look."

I swung the file around and flipped the mug prints over. "This Duke Cerise?"

"That's the name on the folder. You seen him lately?"

"Yeah," I said, "I have."

"In what circumstances?"

"Just standing on a sidewalk talking to a dame."

Wagner said, "It's like opening clams, huh, Larry?'

"Yeah," I said. I looked again at the police print. Sure enough the guy on record was the guy in the bow tie, the guy I'd seen with Carol Weiler.

I closed the file, unclipped my ballpoint and in the space reserved for current details, scored out the car registration number and wrote over it the number I'd taken from the maroon-colored Caddy.

"What's that you're doing?" Wagner's tone was sharp.

I showed him.

He glanced at it, then looked at me, his eyes wary. "You know the guy this well, you know his auto number?"

"I just took it. Force of habit, but—it could be useful data."

"Anything's useful," growled Wagner. "Only this Duke Cerise—he's playing it straight. We've got nothing on him. Why would we be worried over his auto number or any other damn thing about him?"

"What happens to the old mobsters?" I asked him. "Do they fade away?"

"Some of them go legit," he shrugged, "and some of them go West. Open up on the Californian coast, start life anew." He grinned mirthlessly. "Or some of them are deported and wind up in some Italian villa sunning themselves and thinking about the old days." He reached for the phone again.

I said, "Make it fast, Wagner. I got a plane to catch."

"Not yet you haven't." He spoke to someone on the phone and hung up again. "Larry, why are you going to Havana?"

"I'm commissioned to go down there and find a guy."

"Who for?"

"J. B. Weiler."

"Who's the guy?"

I hesitated.

"Come on, let's have it."

"It's not in your department, Wagner."

"I'm a cop, remember?"

"Yeah. Homicide detail. Say, you got your hands full figuring out this new gangland killing. Leave the Havana business with me and I'll call you if anything breaks."

"Your generosity gets me," Wagner growled. "Damned if I won't take you off that plane, just for the hell of it."

I said, "This is the score: Weiler's sending me to Havana to find this guy. In the process I get alongside Albanesi and maybe tie up this dope chain into which Gondola must fit, and maybe where my buddy Jim Calloway fitted, too. Also somewhere in that chain, I might find the dame who was supposed to be the cause of the quarrel and the killing. I'm kind of stubborn over this."

"Calloway's dead," said Wagner bluntly. "No matter what you turn up you can't bring him back to life again."

"You couldn't be more right. But there are some things a guy just can't help doing, in spite of all. Now, you got anything more to ask me?"

He snapped, "You had any other contact since last night with Gondola or any of his bunch?"

I shook my head.

"Been no attempts on your life, anything like that?"

"Nothing."

He grunted.

The phone purred and he picked up the receiver, identified himself. "Uh-huh? ... Yeah ... I see ... Okay, lieutenant, make a routine check with airline offices, the port authority. How's that? No, no, we don't have anything on him right now. Just routine."

He hung up.

"This contact of yours, this Gus Elsinore, he checked out of the

Columbus Hotel first thing this morning." Wagner pursed up his lips. "Could be he's gone down the river."

"Could be," I admitted.

"Or maybe even gone down to Havana, Cuba."

"You figure everybody is headed that way?"

"I don't figure anything right now," replied Wagner.

The phone rang again and he said tiredly, "Larry, you take over my job. I go to Havana ... Wagner talking! Oh, yeah. Sure, I get it. Thanks a lot." He hung up.

I looked at him.

"Duke Cerise," he said tersely. "In the last three years he's been president of a shipping agency operating on Lower Wall Street. He has an apartment on Columbus Circle, and a country house on Long Island Sound. He's well-heeled for chips, and he hasn't put a foot wrong since that income-tax rap. Next question."

"Guess there aren't any," I said, and reached for my hat.

"You going to leave it that way, Larry?"

"How else do I leave it? If anything breaks, I'll call you, Wagner."

"You know something, Larry?"

"Yeah?"

"I'm in two minds about you."

"Extravagant guy."

"Maybe I should stop you from flying out today, for the sake of your health, huh?"

I flipped a hand at him. "Take care of your end of things and—send a wreath from me to Johnny Omar's funeral. A hand cut wreath."

4

Fly high, baby ...

I checked my baggage through at La Guardia and carrying a light grip in my hand, moved through to the concourse. A guy touched my arm. I turned quickly. He was wearing a uniform jacket with the emblem of the airfield on the lapel.

"Are you Mr. Larry Kent?"

"Yeah."

"They want you at the Customs' Office."

"What for?"

"I wouldn't know, bud. I only work around here."

I glanced up at the clock on the wall. It wanted fifteen minutes to take-off time.

"Okay," I said. "Where do I go?"

"I'll show you, mister." He turned and headed quickly away through the crowd.

I followed him. As I walked I transferred the grip to my left hand. The uniformed guy led the way round the side of a block of offices at the end of the concourse. He paused for a moment, turned and beckoned me on, then disappeared round back of the freight section. When I got there he was looking about him.

I said, "What's the grief?"

"Just wait right here," he said, and dived down a corridor that led away from the freight-loading alley.

I was about to go after him when a voice from behind me said, "Hold it right there, bud."

I put my right hand into the pocket of my overcoat.

The voice said, "Don't move. Pull anything and you're a dead duck."

I stood very still. There came the sound of quick footsteps and somebody grabbed my right arm above the elbow. I looked down at him. It was the guy who had come into the restaurant with the message for Carol Weiler from Duke Cerise. From behind me the voice that had spoken before said, "I got a gun on you, Kent. Don't make any trouble or I'll have to use it on you."

The guy holding me by the arm pushed me forward. "Start walking," he said.

I walked.

A couple of men hurried past us, dressed in the airport uniform that the first guy had been wearing. They didn't even glance our way.

Then we were clear of the loading alley and I saw a big covered truck with tailgate down, backed up against the loading bay. The guy who had got me round there on the pretext of seeing the Customs, came into view, carrying a large grip, which he threw into the back of the truck, and then stepped to one side.

"Make it look natural," said the guy holding my arm. "Climb right in."

"Or else," said the guy back of me, and suddenly I felt something prod into the base of my spine.

I moved forward, still holding the small grip in my left hand.

"In you get."

I hesitated only for a moment. I glanced about me. There was quite a lot of bustle and activity further down the bay, but those guys round there weren't interested in anything but their own chores. Mentally I shrugged. I wondered how long they would hold the southbound plane for me. I took my right hand out of my pocket and laid it on the back of the truck and jumped up.

The guy beside me released his grip and scrambled up after me. Then came the sound of the other guy behind, getting in.

"Stand very still."

I stood. I heard the tailgate being slammed into position then the doors were swung to, and I heard the snap of the catch as they joined.

"Okay, relax."

I turned round. A tall, thin, swarthy guy with a blue chin was regarding me coldly. He had a travelling rug over his left arm, smothering the right hand, from which jutted an automatic pistol.

This guy said, "Okay, back up against the wall."

I stumbled in the semi-darkness over to the side of the truck and leaned there.

"Silvie," said the dark guy, "frisk him."

The other one moved in close, taking care not to mask the gun that was held on me. He patted me down scientifically and relieved me of my .32. As he stepped back, he said, "This guy was huntin' bear. Too bad."

The dark one paid no attention to him. His eyes were on me the whole time. He said, "You flying out to Havana?"

"That's right."

"You want to catch that plane?"

"That's the general idea."

"Okay, then. Talk fast."

"About what?" I put an aggrieved tone into my voice. "If this is a stick-up why not get it over with? I've got a few hundred bucks on me. Take it and let me go. I've got a date with that plane."

The swarthy guy said, "Who are you kiddin'?" He moved in close, holding the automatic in a businesslike way. He had shed the travelling rug, and stood lightly balanced on the balls of his feet.

"I'm Gondola." He paused as if to let the big announcement sink in. When I said nothing he went on, "I was a friend of Danny Harbin's. You had him netted and then burnt. A guy oughta kill you slow."

"Okay," I said. "Go right ahead if it's going to make you feel good."

The other one interjected. "Why fool around, Whitey? You know we can't bump him here. For one thing we can't park here all day—"

"Cut it," snapped Gondola, his dark eyes never wavering from my face. "We can get you any time we like, Kent. We can kill you slow or fast just the way we want it. Only—you know something? We're going to let you fly out to Havana. Have your little fun. Havana's a better place for you to get lost in. What do you say?"

"You're wasting your time, Gondola."

His dark eyebrows went up. "So you're going to play it tough?" He half-turned his head. "Okay, Silvie, go out there and tell them at the desk that Larry Kent has cancelled his passage."

"Hold it," I said, before the other guy could move. "What is it you're wanting to know?"

"Now you're being smart," said Gondola. "You weren't satisfied with putting the finger on Danny Harbin, you had to go out there and torment the poor guy before he got burnt." The automatic weaved a little in his hand as if he had clutched it too tightly. "Okay, so you're tough. So you went out there and talked with Danny, and he spilled. What did he spill, Kent?"

I was waiting for just that. Harbin's bunch had sold themselves the idea that he would crack under the strain of the death cell. They knew I had extra-official powers, and that I'd seen him, for sure. In their book it could only mean one thing—that Harbin had been ready to talk and I'd listened to him.

I said, "Sure I saw Harbin. He had plenty to say but none of it made sense." Which, to a point, was the truth.

Gondola snarled, "Not good enough, Kent. You proved yourself a liar by taking on this job for J. B. Weiler. Harbin talked. What did he tell you?" The automatic was rammed into my stomach.

I looked at Gondola. I said, "I could string out a line of lies that would maybe satisfy you, and still catch that plane, but where's the sense? You're getting no place, Gondola, and neither am I."

"Talk, damn you!"

"Harbin told me nothing I didn't know before. That's all I've got to say."

The guy called Silvie exploded, "Slap him down a little, Gondola. What in hell does it matter if he catches that plane or not? Work him over, and we'll take him outa town and—"

"Cut it, I told you, Kent, you were kinda interested personal in the Calloway killing, weren't you?"

I said nothing and he went on, "It was your buddy got killed, and two or three have told me how you swore you'd get the guy who did it. Okay, so you got Danny Harbin. Whether he did it or not I wouldn't know, but I do know this. Danny had a lot of friends."

"You're wasting time, Gondola."

"You're still sticking your nose in that case," he persisted. "You want to know what made Calloway tick, who was the dame back of him, and just why Harbin came into the picture. Well, you play it along our way, and maybe we'll answer a lot of those questions for you. Now what do you say?"

"Sounds quite a deal. Go to hell."

Gondola said, "A guy's crazy, trying to make deals with private eyes." He glanced swiftly at his watch. "You got three minutes to spill it all, or we'll do like Sylvie says and work you over and kill you later. What's it to be?"

To a point he was bluffing. He had no means of knowing how much Harbin had told me, and—for some big reason he was keen that I fly out to Havana. Same time, he was getting no place fast, and he knew it and I knew it.

By the same token there was nothing I could say that would pacify Gondola at that stage. It was futile—like slugging at shadows.

I said, "You're crowding me, Gondola. Ease up."

"Time's running out—"

"Sure," I said. "Who cares about that plane? There are plenty of planes."

He looked at me for a moment, then moved back from me, his gun still lined up on my stomach.

"Silvie," he began, but got no further.

I swung my left wrist in a short arc that looped the small grip over and down in a chopping motion, slamming down on his gun hand. As the grip made contact, I slugged Gondola hard across the bridge of the nose with the flat of my palm.

Things happened fast after that.

I kicked Gondola before he hit the floor of the van. As Silvie, his mouth open with shock, fumbled for the gun under his coat, I stooped and picked up Gondola's gun, reversed it and slammed the butt flush against the side of Silvie's temple. He shot sideways, hit the wall of the van, rolled over and lay still.

I glanced at Gondola who was writhing, making moaning noises. I went over to Silvie, stooped and retrieved my .32. I dropped a gun in each side pocket, retrieved my grip, went to the rear door. I banged on it sharply and it opened at once, widely enough to show the face of the phony guy in uniform. Before he could speak I crowded through the entrance, falling on top of him.

He gave a yelp, slumping like a bag of sawdust. I grabbed him, propped him upright, said into his sagging face, "You're going with me to the plane. Your pals pull anything and you'll be the first one to get it." He was gobbling with fear.

I walked him briskly up through the alley, past the freight section and on to the concourse. Loudspeakers were announcing the departure of my plane. I looked about me but could see no sign of Carol Weiler. Then, as we walked out the promenade deck, I had a glimpse of a sharply-dressed balding man standing smoking a cigar, a little apart from the crowd.

Duke Cerise. He didn't even turn his head.

We were on the windy tarmac. It wanted a couple of minutes before noon. I turned to the little guy.

"Okay, beat it."

He gave me one look and fled.

I went aboard the plane. As I checked in and took my seat alongside Carol Weiler, she turned and said, "I thought you were never coming."

She sounded cold.

The big transcontinental plane took off on its first long leg of the flight south.

***

We didn't talk much on that first leg. Carol seemed to be preoccupied with her own thoughts, and me—I was trying to figure how a luscious, luxury-lapped dame like this one could get tangled with a one-time mobster like Duke Cerise. From a photographer's point of view Carol was all dame—she stacked up structurally to the fan's idea of a perfect woman. She was tall—slim—her blue eyes set off by those intriguing dark eyebrows flying away at the corners to give her a faintly surprised look, like she was amused at the world and men in particular.

I'm not a photographer.

Maybe what I needed to be was a psychiatrist. One of those guys who get a dame to loll on a couch and give with her dreams. It always struck me as soft touch—this analyzing of dames with worries on their mind. But maybe I had it wrong way round. I was the guy who was worrying, and Carol—that crazy mixed-up millionaire's daughter—was the one who seemed like she didn't have a care in the world. We talked.

We covered the weather, we covered the airline service. We even shared a baby-bottle of Scotch together. She told me a little about her old man but not much. She skated around any serious topic and when I got onto the subject of Rock Alison she wasn't all that communicative.

In other words, she didn't give any more than a fast pick-up at a polo-game.

So we changed planes and flew on, after a meal which I ate alone in the airport restaurant. Carol vanished and didn't show up again until take-off time. I didn't comment on her sudden disappearance and she didn't volunteer any information.

A dame with more reserve than the Chase National Bank.

All flights come to an end sometime, and we touched down at Havana early in the morning. So early the nightclub moochers hadn't yet thought about setting a course for home. Carol had spent the last three hours reclining back in her sleeperette seat, her rug draped casually over her magnificent legs. In that time I used up a lot of gray matter trying to figure the pieces together. J. B. Weiler was big-time. He had a representative in Havana, Rock Alison and that guy and Carol, the boss's daughter were that way about each other. So this Rock Alison gets himself lost, and Weiler does plenty of worrying. It was at this point in my reasoning I figured Weiler *was* straight in his dealings with Havana. At the same time he was plenty concerned about not getting mixed up in any dope scandal. On account of a bad mistake he once made.

Now it shows on the screen that his ever-loving daughter is so thick with onetime gangster, Duke Cerise, that he's even at the airport when she takes off.

And then I get the shakedown treatment.

Coincidence?

I would be willing to bet dollars to pesos that Duke Cerise masterminded the attempted snatch when the boys put the freeze on me at the airport. Gondola was a stooge, and I was betting that he was on Duke Cerise's payroll.

And yet, according to police records, Cerise had gone straight for years. So what did that prove? Once a mobster, always a mobster? It sure didn't look like that on the record, but still ... There was Danny Harbin, who was supposed to have sounded off to me, before he died. Duke Cerise was plenty interested in the talk I had had with the guy in the condemned cell. So interested that he pulled that snatch at the airport, right out there in the daylight.

My figuring was getting me no place and the dame slept on—or seemed to sleep.

So we were touching down and going through the formalities of leaving the airport, Carol Weiler, having freshened up in the powderroom, looked like several million dollars of Pan-American goodwill.

I waited for her. I wasn't going to let her slip away that easy. Dames who don't talk keep me awake nights. It isn't natural, for one thing, and for another, I like to hear dames talk.

"You're booked in at the Hotel of the Americas?"

She turned limpid blue eyes on me. "Why, yes, Larry."

"Okay. We'll share a cab."

"If you like." Her tone was indifferent.

I said, "Unfreeze, baby. You're in the equatorial zone or didn't you know it?"

She stared at me in silence for a long moment. Then, "I should know. I spend a lot of time down here."

"Great." I went and flagged down a taxi. As I helped her in she said, "The flight's over. Don't get any silly ideas, Larry."

I slammed the door and settled back beside her. As the car slid off toward the center of the New Town I said, "What triggered off that remark?"

"Well—" She shrugged. "It's getting that way we're like an old married couple."

"Is that bad?"

"It could be. After all, I've got strong ideas about who I get around with."

"It was your idea flying down with me. You want to change your ideas now, I'll stop the cab."

I leant forward and she grabbed at my arm.

"Don't be silly."

"Okay," I said. "Why the beef?"

Suddenly she seemed to thaw. She pulled me down beside her and said in a cooing voice, "I got the idea you were mad at me on the flight down."

"It was a long flight."

"Sure, Larry, but was it all that tedious?"

I didn't say anything.

"Larry, are you mad at me?"

"Why should I be?" I felt for cigarettes, offered one to her but she shook her head. I lit one.

She said, "You're keeping something back, aren't you?"

"Yeah," I said. "I guess it's catching."

"Just what do you mean by that?"

"Skip it." I figured it wasn't the time for trading of confidences. I yet had to feel my way with this dame—and her association with Duke Cerise.

The taxi pulled up at the entrance to the hotel and I helped her out, paid off the hackie, then stood by whilst our baggage was shipped into the lobby. By that time the dame had booked in and was waiting with an impatient look on her face for me to register. When I was through she said, "I guess we'll meet in the morning."

"Could be."

"It's morning now, really," said Carol, "but I don't intend to get up until before noon."

"We'll go out together," I told her, "and find your boyfriend."

Her eyes glowed. "If you mean Rock Alison—"

"The guy you're carrying the torch for."

We stood there in the middle of the lobby, facing each other like we were all set for a sparring match.

Carol said, "I'm very much in love with Rock Alison. I'd do just about anything to get him back safe and well." She turned and swept away toward the elevator.

I strolled after her, lighting a fresh cigarette.

We rode up in the elevator together and I said, "Looks like we're on the same floor."

"I told you not to get any wrong ideas."

I jerked my head toward the night-clerk who was working the elevator.

"Not in front of the children," I warned her.

She scowled, stepped out of the elevator, and I went along with her whilst her baggage was taken in. In the doorway, she waited until the porter was through, then leaned against the door frame and said, "All right, let's have it."

I looked at her.

"You're wondering about Duke Cerise, aren't you?"

"Why would I wonder about that guy? A small-time mobster never interested me all that much."

I saw the flush climb slowly up her smooth cheeks.

I said, "See you tomorrow, baby."

"Wait a minute."

I checked and looked at her.

"You're playing this tough, Larry. Look out it doesn't spring back and hit you right in the face."

I said, "All of a sudden you're playing in the opposition league. Is it because you're so far away from home and poppa?"

She said nothing.

I turned and walked down the corridor to my room. The door was open and my bags stood in the room. The porter was waiting. I tipped him, he went out.

I started to unpack. For the first time it hit me that I was dog-weary. And thirsty. I picked up the phone, called room service and ordered a bottle of Scotch and a jug of cracked ice. Then I went to the adjoining shower-room and turned the taps. I was stripping off my shirt, when there was a knock on the door.

"It's unlatched."

The door opened. There was silence. I turned round and Carol Weiler was standing there.

"Oh," she said.

"Come right in," I told her. "If I'd known you were headed this way, I'd have ordered another bottle."

She closed the door firmly behind her and stood leaning against it. She'd taken off the light overcoat she'd worn over her dress on the flight down, but otherwise she was just the same. A little travel-weary but radiant as ever.

"Larry, I want to talk to you."

"Hold it right there," I told her. "I was just about to take a shower."

"I'm sorry about that."

"I bet you are." I walked through, turned off the faucets and went back into the room, tucking my shirt into my pants' top. I went over to the table where the liquor had been placed and fetched another glass for her. "I'm feeling neighborly," I told her. "Maybe it's the Pan-American influence. You know, we've got plenty to gain down here in Cuba. A lot of trade, a lot of goodwill."

"You don't have to go on with that sort of stuff, Larry. I don't really need a drink—"

I handed her the glass.

She took it and sat in the guest chair near the table.

I leaned against the wall with the glass in my hand, and a cigarette smoldering from the other.

Cozy.

"Larry, about Duke Cerise."

"Uh-huh?"

"He's quite a friend of mine."

"So I noticed." Again I saw the storm signal in her eyes, but she choked back whatever she was going to say and instead, "Duke Cerise has been very useful to me."

"Doing what? Giving you an introduction to what the popular Press calls the underworld?"

"Look, Larry, you don't have to give it to me like that. Cerise is quite a guy. He's got a lot of contacts." She paused and added deliberately, "Especially in Havana."

"Uh-huh?"

"In fact he's quite a powerful man, well worth knowing."

"Tell me when to cheer, baby." I took some of my drink.

She moved restlessly on her chair, then said, "I think that he can help me find out where Rock Alison is."

"That so? You know, you had me worried for a while. I figured your old man hired me to find Rock Alison and you were just tagging along for laughs. Now I can see that J. B. Weiler is throwing away his dough. He didn't have to send me down here at all. You could have come under your own steam—and with Duke Cerise's help, found Rock Alison and made your old man happy in one hit. Check me where I go wrong."

"Right there," she said. She got up out of the chair with a swift, fluid motion and faced me. "Listen, Larry, you had to come down here. My father was quite right in sending you. Rock's disappeared, and to get him out of trouble, you'll have to use tactics that wouldn't go down so well in New York. That's why J. B. picked you and he was quite right."

I looked at her, said nothing.

She went on with earnestness in her voice. "There's a big and dirty business being worked down here, although its headquarters are in New York. I believe that Duke Cerise is back of that circus and that's why Rock disappeared because he got wise. He's a straight-shooter, Larry. There isn't a whiter man anywhere than Rock Alison. He was all for J. B. and he was a very useful agent for him. Now, can you see why it's so vitally important to find him?"

"You're giving me nothing new, baby. Lay it on the line."

"I didn't want to do that—this early, but a few minutes ago, after you left my room, I made up my mind I had to talk to you."

"Okay, talk."

She drew a deep breath and linked, her hands together. In her husky, beguiling voice she said, "I believe Rock got wise to this dope ring—found out that someone in the ring had been blackmailing my father because of something that happened years ago. Something to do with dope."

"That figures," I nodded.

"Well, just by chance a few weeks ago I met Duke Cerise at the house of an old friend. It was quite a social affair, and well, you'd be surprised how big a figure Duke Cerise cut among the upper fifty in high financial society."

"Do tell."

"Well, we met." She shrugged. "He seemed to be attracted to me. He asked me to go out with him. I didn't want to, but while he talked with me he let drop a name—and that name linked him with the crowd that Rock had been trying to open up down here in Havana."

"What name would that be, baby?"

"Albanesi."

"That figures, too." Suddenly I was interested. I finished my drink, went over to the table and poured another. I said, "So Cerise let go with Albanesi's name and you started to suspect that he was mixed up in the Havana dope traffic?"

"Yes, Larry; that's it in a nutshell. I played along with Duke Cerise. He was very keen—he even asked me to marry him." She gave a short laugh. "Little does he know that I've used him all along the line."

"You're starting to get phony, Carol," I told her.

She gave an exclamation and her eyes blazed.

"You had me in your audience up to this point, baby. As of now, you're pushing empty air."

She seemed to be fighting for control. At last she said, "You're a heel, Larry Kent."

"Sure," I said. "Have another drink."

"I don't want another drink." She slammed the half empty glass on the table and swung back to me. "I was prepared to help you all I could, now I'm going to let you find your own way around."

"Okay," I said. "That's the way I like it. I'm a guy gets around most times alone."

"You may be sorry for this." She was breathing deeply. And in the process looking more gorgeous than ever. "I shan't be worrying you any further, Larry Kent. Don't ask me for help, that's all. Just don't ask me." She headed for the door.

I let her go that far then said, "Relax. A babe like you should be taking it easy. Plenty cologne and the right kind of company. The hell with Duke Cerise. Have yourself a time."

She swung round and I saw her face was white. "I hate you. I just hate you!" She plucked open the door and swept out, slamming the door behind her.

I shrugged, reached for the Scotch bottle.

Something was wrong some place. Wrong and screwy. I started to wonder if it was maybe me who needed that psychiatrist.

5

Hot time in Havana ...

"Perdonne, señor. You are Larry Kent?"

"That's right."

The little guy bobbed his head, his black eyes merry. "This way, señor. You're expected."

I followed him through the cafe to a back room. It was curtained off, and he twitched the curtain aside, thrust his head in and said something in Spanish. Then he turned back to me, beaming. "Señor." He gave a deep bow, and I hit his hand with a good American buck.

"Gracias, capitan."

"You're promoting me," I told him. I went through the curtain.

A guy got up from the table. He was tall, slim, with dark eyes, a mobile face. He had his hand out-thrust.

"Señor Larry Kent?"

"Yeah." I shook with him.

He said formally, "I'm Rodriguez. At your service."

"Glad to meet you," Rodriguez."

"You may call me Rod," he said, thawing suddenly. Smiling like a schoolboy he indicated a chair and I sat down.

Then the little guy was back with a bottle of white rum which he placed reverently on the table with two fancy glasses.

"Your pleasure, señor?"

"Scotch pleases me more."

The little guy looked crestfallen. "If you would just try this, señor?"

"Scotch," I told him.

He sighed and withdrew.

Rodriguez laughed and poured himself a drink. "You wouldn't hurt Pico's feelings, would you? Try some."

"Okay." I took the glass of rum he thrust toward me and when Pico came back with the bottle of Scotch I told him to put it at arm's reach.

As soon as he had gone Rodriguez leaned toward me, his glass clutched in his hand. His face wore an earnest expression.

"As you know, I'm an agent for the United States Narcotics Bureau. I am many other things besides, señor. For instance, in this cafe I am known as a man who has many connections with the Americans, in the buying and selling of fine liqueurs." He laughed, showing white teeth. "In other places I'm known as other things. That's the way I operate."

"Sounds great." I had some of my rum and nodded. "Tastes great, too. Well, Rod, you got any angles for me?"

"About Rock Alison?"

I looked at him quickly.

He smiled. "I had a cable this morning from Washington."

"They work fast," I told him. "Could it be your cable came from a guy name of Sorenson?"

He nodded. "Washington, it seems, is quite well informed on your movements, Mr. Kent. But I have bad news for you."

I said nothing.

Rodriguez's face was serious as he went on. "As I told you, I've many contacts in this city, but—I have no clue at all as to the whereabouts of Señor Rock Alison."

"That doesn't surprise me any." I leaned back in my chair. "You can give me some information."

"I'm at your service completely, señor."

"You know a man named Albanesi?"

He frowned at once, thinking hard. Then he exclaimed, "There is one Albanesi—"

"One's plenty."

"He's a trader, I believe. Yes—let me think for a moment." He wrinkled his forehead and tapped his hands nervously on the table. Then his face cleared. "Yes, I remember now. There is an Albanesi who spent many years in the United States and London. A much-travelled gentleman. I remember the police checked him once and I was called in—behind the scenes, you know? He was suspected of having imported raw opium into the West Indies. Albanesi cleared himself, but that was—let me see—two years ago."

"Heard anything of him since?"

"Not a thing, señor." His face brightened. "You would like me to find out about Albanesi?"

"Yeah, I'd appreciate that. I'm at the Hotel of the Americas. You could contact me there."

He got to his feet. "Gladly, señor. Is there anything else?"

"Quite a lot. Sit down, Rodriguez."

He sat and waited expectantly.

I told him the score on Duke Cerise, told him I suspected that Cerise was masterminding the U.S. end of the dope ring that operated from Havana.

"Duke Cerise is a one-time mobster who's supposed to have gone straight for years. He's a smooth operator. He has a guy on his payroll name of Gondola. He was in New York last time I saw him, but if there's anything to bring him to Cuba, he'll be in Havana pretty soon, I guess. Now, you tell me this, Rodriguez. From your know-how of the illicit narcotics trade in this town—and your line on Rock Alison—why do you think Duke Cerise and Gondola could be so interested in affairs down here, right now?"

He thought for a moment, then said slowly, "Señor, a big ring operates here. We have been working on it for ten months. We've made little headway, but Rock Alison really got on to something, and I guess that's why he disappeared."

"You think he's dead?"

He shook his head somberly. "I think not. Not that they would stop at murder, but he knows so much that he'll be more valuable to them alive. Well now, señor, it seems to me that Alison is the key; it could be that the ring is planning to make a big killing, then shut up shop." His brown eyes rested on me keenly. "You with me, señor?"

"To a point. I can figure the set-up with Duke Cerise at the New York end, Albanesi at this end, and somewhere in the middle, little guys like Gondola and a dope-pusher by the name of Gus Elsinore. That name mean anything to you?"

He shook his head negatively.

"Elsinore's trying hard to get alongside Albanesi, to make a private deal outside of the New York ring. He was running with Gondola's bunch, but Gondola sold him short, and now Elsinore's anti anything that even touches on Gondola. Seemed to me he was eager to get alongside Albanesi because of a big killing he could smell. Now you can see I'm with you to a point."

Rodriguez said, "I would say more than that." He smiled and poured fresh drinks for us. He checked, with the bottle tilted halfway toward my glass, raised his eyebrows questioningly.

"Go ahead," I told him. "I'm getting the Cuban taste."

"Well, señor—" He settled back in his chair. "I think the big killing is about to come off and that could attract the New York boys. But don't forget that with Rock Alison in their grasp, they hold one big ace, and that makes our work just so much harder."

"I get you." I took some of my drink. "Now about the local cops—"

"I have to go careful with the Havana police," said Rodriguez. "I'm strictly undercover. But if need be, I would come out in the open."

"Would it be possible for you to fix it so I could see the police records on Albanesi?"

"Of course, señor," he said eagerly. "That could be easily arranged."

"Records on Albanesi and mug files on any of his known associates. Also whatever information you've got on the drug ring that has been operating here in the last ten months. Can do?"

"But of course, señor." He smiled, finished off his drink and got to his feet. "I will meet you in the bar of the Hotel of the Americas at—let me see—" He glanced at his watch. "Half-past-three?"

"Suits me fine."

We shook hands.

"Before you leave, señor, speak to Pico and tell him how much you enjoyed our local rum. Yes?"

***

I spent an hour checking the data that J. B. Weiler had given me. When I was through I wondered about Carol. I hadn't seen her since early morning, when she'd left my hotel room. I checked discreetly at the desk, but she had left at the time when I was heading out for my rendezvous with Rodriguez.

I went downstairs to the American Bar and had myself a Scotch and a sandwich.

It was there that Lolita found me.

She slid onto the stool alongside mine, as if we were still back in New York—and the clock had stopped.

"A Martini please, Larry."

I looked at her. She was dark, sloe-eyed, her skin seemed to be bursting with that sort of built-in radiance those Spanish-type dames carry around with them.

"Did I ever tell you I'm crazy over you?"

She smiled, dimpling. She cocked her head at the bartender.

"Please?"

I ordered a Martini, and Scotch for myself. "Well," I said, "this is better than Manhattan in the rain, huh?"

She had her knee against mine as we sat side by side on our stools. She laid her hand on my arm.

"Larry, are you glad I came here?"

"This is where you belong, baby."

"Why do you say that?"

"This is Havana. Your town. I don't have to say more."

"You could say an awful lot more," she said breathlessly. "Only it's very public here, Larry."

"You got any ideas?"

"Plenty."

"Well, then—"

"No!" She gave a rueful laugh. "Business first."

"Okay," I said. "Give with the business."

She took a sip of her drink, then said, "J. B. Weiler must trust you very much, to send you all the way down here to find Rock Alison."

"You were the one who sweet-talked me into it, remember?"

"Yes, I know." She shook her head impatiently. "But New York is so far from here, and J. B. Weiler doesn't realize just what goes on, do you think?"

"I don't think anything right now. I'm anaesthetized. What's that perfume you're wearing? King-size Chanel 5?"

She laughed, her long, white throat moving.

I had a sudden crazy desire to bite that throat. I checked myself and had some of my Scotch.

Lolita said, "This is Havana. And here you are looking for Rock Alison and Larry, what are you doing about Carol Weiler?"

"So it's that way, huh?"

"It isn't that way at all. I only know that she talked her father into letting her come down here with you, and Larry, I'm awfully jealous."

"If it makes you feel any better baby, I haven't seen her in hours."

"She's just down the bar," said Lolita tartly.

I twisted around on my stool. Sure enough there was Carol Weiler down the bar, and with her was a big, paunchy middle-aged guy beaming at her, feeding her liquor.

I looked at Lolita. She was dimpling again. "Carol Weiler makes time with my father."

"Your father?"

"That is Señor Albanesi. Ask about him in this town, Larry, and you'll find he's a very well-respected man indeed."

I took some more of my Scotch.

"Carol thinks the world of him. He's been J. B. Weiler's agent for years. A very trustworthy man."

There was a mocking quality in her voice I didn't like. I didn't like it a bit. I said, "It would be an idea meeting this Albanesi."

"Why not? He's my father."

"Not as beautiful as you, baby."

She laughed again. "Larry you are the great kidder."

"Yeah," I said. "So Carol thinks he's a very trustworthy agent, huh?"

"But of course. So does her father. But don't let's meet them yet. Let them drink together and talk. Larry, you came here to find Rock Alison. What progress have you made?"

"A whole lot," I told her. If I was lying, I guess I didn't let it show in my voice. "You know something, baby? This is a mighty big town."

"Bigger than you thought it would be, Larry?" Again her tone was mocking.

"Yeah," I said. "Big and tough." I slid off my stool. "You coming now?"

"You might at least wait until I've finished my drink."

"Okay, I'm waiting."

She took some more of her drink then put her glass down impatiently. As she slid off her stool I said, "Where are you staying?"

"At my father's house, just out of town."

"I'll call you."

"Why not?" Her breasts moved uneasily under the thin frock she was wearing. It was a hot day, but Lolita looked cool.

I said, "I'll be seeing you, baby."

"Wait, Larry."

"Well?" I half-turned to face her.

"You want to meet my father, don't you?"

"There'll be plenty times."

"Larry—" She hesitated.

"Yeah?"

"Nothing. So long, Larry."

"So long, chiquita."

Looked like Cuba was getting me.

***

I had one hour before my meet with Rodriguez. I went to an address given me by J. B. Weiler and drew a blank. I tried another address and drew another blank.

I had a drink in a small cafe in the lower end of the Prado. I talked with the bartender but he was what the writing guys call unproductive.

I left that place and went uptown in a cab and took a look at the Morro Castle. It wasn't just a rubberneck's visit; I knew there was a cantina not far away that was patronized by the sort of guys Rodriguez would be interested in; smalltime, but maybe useful.

I found myself in the middle of a bunch of sweating guys who talked a lot, volubly, and drank a lot of vino. I ordered a tequila just for the hell of it—and to try and draw the bartender out.

"Americano?" He beamed at me. A friendly guy with a squint, which was disconcerting in a bartender.

"Sure," I said. "I'm just looking around, taking in the local sights."

He laughed. "You see the fort?"

"Sure. Fine place."

"I'm glad you like it, señor."

"Now," I said, "you give me a Scotch."

He raised his eyebrows and shrugged. "Maybe it won't sit so well with tequila."

"Too bad," I told him. I waited till he poured the Scotch and told him to add the ice. As I took the glass from him, I said, "She's all yours, brother."

He took the bill, squinted at it, then laughed again. "The Americano's rich, generous."

"Sure," I said. "I guess I'm on my own in this bar."

"Señor?"

"Not many Americans round here!"

"Not here. They go to the bars on the other side." He pointed expressively. "This place not good enough for the Americano tourists."

"I'm not looking for tourists," I told him.

"You are looking for someone, then?"

I shrugged. "You know how it is. Just about anybody who talks my lingo would do. Just so he isn't a tourist, you know?"

The bartender scowled at me, then winked—a frightening display from a squint-eyed guy. "The señor is looking for something perhaps to take home. A—shall I say—a souvenir?"

His tone was so conspiratorial I nodded, before I could stop myself.

He said, "A little black-market something, or—" He broke off. "Your pardon, señor." He moved down the bar to serve another customer and I sipped thoughtfully at my Scotch."

The next moment the bartender was back. "Maybe I could help you, señor."

"Maybe you could."

"There's a man who comes in sometimes. He has things to sell. If you come back around four o'clock I could point him out to you."

"Thanks. Meantime, here's to Cuba."

"Wonderful." He laughed, showing blackened teeth. Then he stopped laughing. He leaned toward me. "There's an Americano just came in but I don't know about him."

I didn't turn round. "Who is he?"

"I don't know his name. He was in here early this morning. I think he has a room hereabouts." He made a grimace of distaste. "Not a rich Americano. Not a tourist."

"Where is he now?"

"Just down the bar, on your right."

I turned slowly.

Gus Elsinore, in person.

***

I tapped him on the shoulder and he froze like he'd been filleted.

"Relax," I told him. "You're among friends."

He whipped his head round and recognizing me, smiled. "Well, what do you know?"

"Yeah," I said. "It's a small world." I pushed a guy aside and got close to Elsinore. "What you doing around here?"

"Just looking. What brings you here, Kent?"

"Just looking."

He laughed again. "Okay, what are you drinking?"

"You buying?"

"Why not?"

"I heard it said you weren't too free with your dinero."

"Would you be? Listen, brother, I'm scratching way down at the bottom of the barrel." His tone was aggrieved. "Look, Kent, I wanted to talk with you, and it looks like fate's been kind all of a sudden."

"Uh-huh? How about that drink?"

"All right, all right." He waved impatiently to the bartender, who came along with a disapproving look on his face and took our orders. When he was out of earshot, Elsinore said, "You made any time with Albanesi?"

"You're throwing the names around, aren't you?"

"Well, why not? None of these wops know English."

A guy right behind him turned round and said, "What did you say, mister?"

Elsinore glanced at his feet.

I laughed. "Meet me in a half-hour at the Domino Bar on the Prado. Got it?"

"Sure, sure." He looked uneasy. "Look, Kent—"

"Save it," I told him. I went out feeling the bartender's eyes on me.

I walked down the hill in the hot sunshine. I remembered my rendezvous with Rodriguez and—I figured that I was getting no place fast. I was so busy with my own thoughts that I didn't notice the car that snaked up behind me, cruised almost to a stop at the curb. The next thing I knew the guy was tapping me on the arm. "Excuse, señor."

I turned quickly. He was young, slim, innocent looking.

"Your name Kent?"

"Uh-huh."

"You left something back there in the bar—"

I looked at him, then glanced back up the hill. "Left something?"

"Yes, señor, but we have it for you, right here in the car." His tone was breathless, urgent. I could hear alarm bells ringing. My right hand must have crept towards my jacket.

He said, "I wouldn't if I were you, señor."

I froze and then looked up the hill and down again. There were plenty passers-by, traffic thick on the road, but I could see no sign of life in the car. And yet I knew …

The slim, young guy said, "You're covered, Señor Kent. You will come to the car, please. Make no trouble."

"Sure," I said. I reached out quickly and grabbed him by the lapel and swung him between me and the car. I held him there and saw his dusky color change to a chalky white, his eyeballs starting.

I said, "I'm a stranger in this town. That means I'm ready to take a chance on just about anything, but I'm not getting into that auto with you, brother."

"Señor Kent," he stuttered.

"Yeah," I said. "Tell the boyfriends that I'm still around and I aim to stay that way."

I walked him backward across the sidewalk then flung him toward the car and jumped sideways, leaping in back of a parked car, as the guy inside the auto cut loose with a silenced automatic. It made a dull, chopping sound as the bullet churned across the sidewalk and buried itself in the front of a hardware store shaded against the glare, somber in the sunlight.

Then I was two cars away and crouching. Right then I wasn't letting myself get ventilated in Havana, not in broad daylight, not before I'd talked again with Carol Weiler.

I saw the auto snaking out from the curb, heading down the hill, fast.

I got out from back of the parked car, dusted myself down. I walked on to the Domino Bar and had myself a Scotch. Then I had myself another one. I was starting to relax when Gus Elsinore came in. He was looking about him nervously as he entered, and as soon as he came up to me, he said, "Kent, I don't like this one bit."

I looked at him. "You don't like it? You should have been around a few minutes back."

"How come?" He squeezed himself onto a stool, his face scowling.

I said, "A lot of guys are busy round this town, Elsinore. Some of them could be ex-friends of yours."

He shot a quick look at me. "Meaning?"

"You talk, huh?"

"Okay, okay, just so long as I get close to Albanesi—"

I said, "Choke it off." I nodded to the bartender who came along just then. "What you drinking?"

Elsinore said thoughtfully, "I'll have myself a beer." The drinks came.

I said, "We'll take them over to that table."

Elsinore padded after me quietly and I sat down and he sat opposite me.

I said, "Okay, so you want to get alongside Albanesi. I can fix that for you."

His face lightened. "Okay, so I didn't come down to Havana for nothing."

"Look, Elsinore, you've been pushing dope for a good many years and you got away with it. Would it surprise you to know that I put the cops wise to you before I left New York?"

He shook his head vigorously. "It wouldn't surprise me any. I've been on the fringe for a long time. I played along with Gondola because—well it suited me that way. But his methods were too high-pressure for me and I bought out. Of course, the fact that he double-crossed me a little didn't help at all—"

"Skip it," I told him, "I don't want your troubles, Elsinore. What I want from you is straight birdseed. Who was Calloway's dame?"

"Are you kidding?" His eyes were big. "That's dead stuff. Look—I told you I wanted Albanesi so I could make a deal with him. You know something? That guy's the biggest, hottest guy this side of the equator. I heard tell he was needing new blood in New York, new agents to push his stuff for him. That's why I wanted to make the deal. I figured you was in the inside."

"Yeah," I said. "Sure I'm in. But I came down here for one purpose and you're going to help me out."

"How wrong can you get? I don't help at all."

I reached out, grabbed his hand and bent it back against his wrist.

His face went white.

I said, "Elsinore, I'm playing for keeps. You don't know Albanesi but you know plenty of other guys. I want you to take me to those other guys."

He licked his lips. "Please, Kent."

"Okay," I said. "Let's have it."

"If I—if I spill plenty, will you help me out—with Albanesi?"

"I'll help you in hell."

"Then, we can't talk—hell, a man's got to make a living, hasn't he?"

"Why?" I put more pressure on his hand and he squealed. I let him go.

"Finish your beer," I told him.

He drank thirstily.

I said, "This is bigger than you, and it's bigger than me, too, Elsinore. Put me wise or I'll have you extradited and cooled in Sing Sing for nine years. Now, what's it to be?"

"You got me on a limb, Larry." He mustered up a smile. "You know, all along I knew I was wrong when I bucked Gondola."

"On account of Duke Cerise is behind Gondola?"

He looked around swiftly. His mouth was pouting in protest.

I said, "Okay, so what? Nobody can hear us."

"I'm scared. For the first time, I'm scared."

"I bet you are," I told him. "Duke Cerise is back of Gondola and he's masterminding this drug ring. Danny Harbin was on his payroll—" I leaned forward suddenly, so suddenly that he blanched back.

"Where did Jim Calloway fit, Elsinore?"

"I don't know," he whispered.

"Where did he fit, Elsinore?"

"I tell you I don't know—"

I leaned back slowly in my chair. I said, "Okay, you're going to put me alongside some guy in this town who might have known the dame that Calloway knew."

"Larry," he whispered, "I told you all through I was for you, I was against Gondola. I broke with Gondola. I put you wise, didn't I?"

I said nothing.

"Okay, if you want to get that dame who Calloway fell for, the dame that got him into trouble with Danny Harbin, and Danny Harbin killed him, and you had Harbin killed—"

"Who is she, Elsinore?"

"Lolita," said Gus Elsinore.

***

He had given me the address of an operator, small time, strictly Havana, American-speaking. This guy, Elsinore assured me, could be a lead.

He was.

A dame opened the door. She was short, slight, sultry. She rolled her eyes at me, smiled and licked her lips.

"Can I do anything for you?"

"Sure," I said. "But not right now."

The smile vanished.

I said, "I'm looking for a guy named Esteban."

"He isn't home right now—"

I pushed my way past her and she protested, clutching the robe more tightly around her body. I kicked the door to behind her.

I said, "Where is he?"

"Back there." She jerked her head.

"Okay." I patted her shoulder. "Relax, can't you?"

"I'll call the cops—"

I whipped round on her. "Okay, start calling."

She cringed back.

I went on down the hall, parted a bead curtain and there was a guy sitting at a table playing demon solitaire. He didn't look up.

I said, "Esteban?"

"I'm Esteban."

"I'm Larry Kent."

"So what?"

"I came down here to find a guy."

"Did you find him yet."

"Not yet."

"Well, don't bother me, mister. I got my own troubles."

"Sure," I said. I went over and kicked the table over and the cards went scattering like leaves from an autumn tree.

Esteban leapt to his feet. His hand clawed at his wrist. I kicked out and found his kneecap and he sagged toward me, crying out. I slapped him across the throat and he gagged and fell among the wreckage of the card table.

The dame was clawing at my neck. I got her and held her and suddenly she wilted against me. With her mouth open she said, "Don't hit me."

I said, "It would be easy." I thrust her back and she fell into a chair.

I waited until Esteban got to his feet. He wasn't reaching for the knife at his wrist any more. I held a gun right on his stomach.

"Okay, Esteban, where is he?"

"Where's who?"

"Norge."

Esteban shook his head slowly. "I haven't seen him in months."

"You're lying, Esteban."

"Okay, so I'm lying. You prove it."

I went forward and slapped him across the face.

He took it once, he took it twice, and the third time he reared up against me.

"Okay," I said. "Fight."

Then he sagged.

From the chair the dame said shrilly, "Tell him what he wants to know. Why get pushed around by this big punk?"

Without turning I said, "You're learning American fast, baby. Okay, Esteban, where's Norge?"

He gave me an address. He added, "He'll kill me for this."

"Would I worry?"

"I wouldn't know, mister, but—are you an American Fed?"

"No," I said, "I just want to find a guy."

"Not Norge?"

"No," I said. "A guy name of Rock Alison."

He digested it, then smiled slowly. He straightened, dusting off his clothes. "A moment ago," he said formally, "I would have knifed you gladly, señor, now—I don't know."

"Why don't you know?"

"Because maybe I feel the heat is too much." He glanced across at the dame in the chair. "Maybe I take my little chiquita and we try some other place."

"A good idea," I told him. I stepped closer to him. "Norge is just another guy in my book. He's just one of these small pieces that fits into a machine. You want to make my journey happier by telling me who runs the machine?"

Esteban smiled, "You're a strong man, señor, and very impulsive. If I tell you will you promise to go away from here quickly, and—give me an hour to get my chiquita out of town?"

I said, "I don't make deals with bums."

He shrugged, "Then maybe you'll drink with me?"

"You got it fixed to slip me a mickey finn?"

He rounded on me. "Señor, I'll tell you something. Ever since I heard that Rock Alison had been taken and put away out of sight, I was worried, I was afraid. I knew it was the wrong thing to do. Well—" He shrugged. "Now you've proved it. You'll find Norge, and if you live that long, you'll find Rock Alison. But whatever happens, whatever way it goes, it'll be bad luck for me. Therefore I say, God go with you, señor."

"Fair enough." I nodded to him, turned to the dame. "Thanks a lot, baby."

She leapt to her feet. "I wouldn't do it if I were you, señor."

"Wouldn't do what?"

"Go after Norge."

I shrugged.

Behind me Esteban said, "I have a bottle here. Drink with us, señor."

"Okay. Pour it."

The dame stood beside me, smiling, whilst her boyfriend poured the drinks. The heat made the room drowsy. In back of us was the heavy drumming of a fan.

Esteban held a glass out to me. "I cannot say we are friends, señor—but I like the way you fight."

I nodded and took the glass and drank.

Esteban and the dame drank with me.

I said, "I'll give you two hours to get out of town."

Immediately Esteban reached for the bottle. "All along, I know you were a good man, señor. You have the right heart in you. Here, here." He slopped more liquor into my glass.

"Take it easy," I told him. "This climate's getting me down."

He laughed, and the dame laughed with him, then she clutched at my arm.

"I think you are wonderful," she cooed.

Esteban said disgustedly, "Women! You give them everything and they want more."

I finished my drink and put down the glass. Then I patted the dame on the seat.

"Look out for him," I told her. "And remember, when those two hours are up, this town's going to be loaded against you two."

Esteban hurried after me to the door. As I opened it, he said, "Tell Norge you've come from Albanesi."

"And then?"

His mouth was open as he thought fiercely and then he said, "Tell him Duke Cerise is ready to make a deal with Albanesi."

"That's good talk, Esteban."

"Whoever sent you here, sent you to the right man." He jerked his head back toward the dame. "Start packing, beloved. We leave inside an hour."

6

Fat and lean, they die quick ...

I went back to the hotel and there was Rodriguez waiting. I had a drink with him in my room. He showed me the police file on Albanesi. After a time I gave him the lowdown on my movements. Then I said. "Get your operatives to close in on Albanesi. I'll follow up Norge, try and get alongside the guys who are holding Rock Alison. This is it, Rodriguez."

His face was set, determined. "I don't like it at all," he said abruptly.

I glanced at him curiously. "Say, what you want? A satin-lined coffin?"

"Larry—if I may call you that: I think it's time we called in the City Police."

"You do as you like about that."

He looked relieved at once. Then, "I may make this official?"

"Until now," I told him, "you've made it your own way. You're an agent for the U.S. Federal Government, remember?"

"Yes," he said. "But now it is different. I think there will be a great deal of trouble."

"Okay," I said. "So there'll be trouble. You play it any way you like, Rodriguez, only—I work this out my own way."

We stood up together. He put out his hand impulsively, and I shook it.

"Keep contact."

We went out together.

I took a cab.

***

It was a long, cool house, white-painted, with pillars at the front and a phony air of respectability about it.

I went not to the front door, but the side. I rang the bell and after a long wait, a native woman in a white uniform opened the door.

"Señor Norge?"

She shook her head vacantly.

I said, "I've come from Albanesi. Tell him."

She went away and I waited some more. Through the half-open door I could see a dimly-lit hall. It was late in the afternoon, and the heat was still hanging like a shroud about that town.

The dame was back and a guy with her. A small, dark eyed, alert guy.

He said, "What's your trouble?"

"I'm from Albanesi."

"Come in."

I went in. The door closed behind me. The guy said something in Spanish to the dame and she went away at once. He said to me with a smile, "Norge wasn't expecting you."

"I guess he wasn't."

"All right. Come through."

I went through, down the hall, and by a side door into a room whirring with fans. A guy sat drinking at a table. He looked up and said, "Who are you, anyway?"

"The name's Larry Kent."

"Where from?"

"New York City."

He sat back in his chair, a fat, gross guy. The sweat was beaded on his face. "You said you were from Albanesi?"

"That's right." I was aware of the other guy standing right behind me, expectantly. I said, "Norge, I want Rock Alison."

For a long moment nothing was said in that room. Then the big guy hoisted himself to his feet. He said with a sort of chuckle in his voice, "Who in hell are you, anyway?"

"Just a guy."

"Take him, Peter."

I heard a movement behind me, whipped round and slapped the slim guy's wrist before he had time to even reach for his gun.

I had my hand on my gun butt. I said, "Play it tough, Norge, and you'll get it that way."

The fat guy looked at me, as immobile as a cigar-store Indian. He said, "You've got your gall coming here, asking for Alison."

"And you're taking me to him."

"The hell I am."

I took out my gun. I whipped it around in my hand and clubbed the young guy on the side of the head. He crumpled without a sound. As he hit the floor, the fat guy said, "I'll have you killed for this."

"Start it." I moved in on him.

His hands suddenly fumbled at the table and I kicked it against his belly. He groped at me with empty hands. I thrust the gun right under his heart.

"All right, Norge. This is my play. You just go for the ride, huh?"

His face was ashen.

"Alison, remember? We're going there. You're taking me."

"I don't have to take you far," he mouthed. "Sure, you can see Alison. You can talk with him. You can even take him away. Only—you kill me, Kent, and this whole town'll fall right about your ears."

With my free hand I reached up and slapped him across the mouth. He stumbled back, stuttering curses.

I said, "You started this, Norge. Carry it right through."

He turned and stumbled from the room. I was close on his heels. He opened the door, walked down a passage and opened another door. Then he paused and turned on me, fat and limp in his white ducks.

"Albanesi, you said?"

"Sure," I told him easily. "The ring's falling apart, didn't you know?" I added, "Did they give you Weiler's fifty grand for snatching Alison?"

He stared at me, then with a sort of shudder of his big frame, turned away. He unlocked another door and threw it wide.

"He's in there."

"You go first, Norge." Then he fell on me. He was quick, but not quick enough. I shot him in the arm. He fell back, squealing, against the door, and I clubbed him in the fat neck so that he fell sideways and then sprawled on the floor silent, face down.

I went into the room, kicking the door wider as I went.

A tall, slim young guy got up from a cot at the far end of the room. There was a big question on his face.

I said, "Rock Alison."

"Yes, but—"

"I'm Larry Kent. I'm acting for J. B. Weiler."

His face cleared at once. He said impulsively, "I knew J. B. wouldn't let me down."

"Okay," I said. "Skip the bouquets. We've got to get out of here fast."

And then I saw he was chained to his bed by an ankle lock and a slim steel chain.

"How in hell do I get this off?"

"Norge has a key."

I went back to the fat guy, stooped over his sprawling body, fumbled and came up with a bunch of keys which I snapped from his suspender. I went back to Alison, tried three keys before I got the right one. Then I had him free. He flexed himself, laughing, a tall, athletic, very American young guy.

I said, "Carol Weiler's waiting for you."

"I knew it."

"Okay," I said. "So you knew it. Did you also know she was running with Duke Cerise?"

The smile faded.

"Okay," I said. "Maybe I didn't have to make it that tough for you. Let's go."

We went back the way I had come. We were in a dozen yards of the side door when a shot spanged down the corridor and Alison lurched against me, clutching at his arm. I whipped round fast, pulled him to one side and fired with my .32. I saw a guy dodge out of sight. Without turning I said, "Keep running, Alison. Run for the Hotel of the Americas. Ask for Larry Kent. Get to my room."

He hesitated for a moment, then plunged out and I saw him holding his left arm stiffly, as if the blood was running down his sleeve.

There were four of them crowded down the end of the passage. We traded shots for a while and then as I backed for the side door, one of them jumped out from cover, firing coolly. There was something familiar about that guy, and as I shot him, I called, "You're way out of your league, Gondola."

He came on toward me in spite of the slug that had gone clear through him. His face was contorted.

"I'll get you for this, shamus."

"Start getting." My gun was slanted against him.

He came on and on, right on top of me, crowding my gun. Then he fell at my feet, dead.

I went out into the sunlight in time to see the rear end of a taxi whirling away toward the town.

There was another taxi on the rank and I took that. As I went I reloaded my gun from the spare shells in my side pocket.

I figured I might need them.

***

Maybe I had underestimated Duke Cerise.

Right on the steps of the Hotel of the Americas, a guy walked up to me. A dark, well-groomed guy with a glint in his eye.

"Larry Kent?"

"Yeah."

"I'm Lieutenant De Silva. Havana Security Police. I'd like you to come along with me."

"Yeah?"

"We've had a complaint about you. We would like you to come down to headquarters and make a statement."

"You kidding?"

"We don't kid, Mr. Kent. I suggest you come along with us."

"Look," I said, "there's a guy in this town by the name of Rodriguez—"

"Never mind him," he broke in. "Will you come, please?" He moved ahead of me across the sidewalk to where a black, official-looking car stood waiting, city plates front and rear and a radio aerial on its roof.

I followed more slowly. I figured by now Rock Alison was safely in my room. The Norge set-up had been unsnarled, the Esteban bolt-hole had been plugged and—the rest could be history. I shrugged as I ducked my head and got into the car.

"Take him quiet," said the voice of Duke Cerise from the front seat. "If he acts up like he's mean, put him to sleep."

The car whirled down the Prado. Either side of me two of Duke Cerise's hoodlums crowded their guns into my sides.

***

Albanesi was big and sweaty. He was also very smooth and he talked like a Harvard graduate.

He walked slowly across a carpet toward me—toward the chair in which I sprawled, taking it easy, because I no longer had the load of my .32 or the gun I had taken from Gondola to weigh me down.

When he was within a couple of paces of me he stopped and folded his arms across his chest.

"You've given us a lot of trouble, Kent."

I said, "Albanesi, the sands have run out."

"That's big talk," he said. "About ten minutes ago, Duke Cerise showed you just how efficient our organization is. A man who looks like a detective and acts like one, a car that has Havana Police Department plates on it—and here you are. Do you think you're ever going to walk out of here alive, Kent?"

"I wouldn't know about that," I told him. "Right now, all I need is a cigarette."

"You won't get one," he responded affably. "Nor a drink. Nor a woman. Nor even a good sleep. Not till we straighten out two, three things about you, Kent."

"Okay," I said, comfortably. I was thinking about Rock Alison back in my hotel room. Thinking about the big fee I would have got from J. B. Weiler if I'd lived that long. I said, "Albanesi, you're a big-time operator and you've double-crossed Weiler and blackmailed him, and worked things your own way for a long time. But you know something, Albanesi? The sands have run out. Just like I said before."

Without turning his head, he said, "Duke, have a couple of your boys work on this guy, will you?"

I looked around.

There were three other guys in the room. One of them was Duke Cerise. He was leaning against the wall, and there was a half-smoked cigar in his hand—just like there'd been in the auto that had brought me. One cool guy.

The other two were yeggs. One fat, the other slim; layabouts, fast on the knuckle, and faster even on the gun.

They moved in on me purposefully.

Duke Cerise said, "Don't make him so he can't talk."

I went backward with the chair.

And then they were on me. I used my feet, and then when I clawed myself upright, I clubbed one of them. The fat one. He fell against the thin one and the two snarled.

But the slim one broke clear and hit me once in the throat. I fought my way back to the wall, and the one who had clubbed me, fumbled in his jacket for a moment, came out with a blackjack that swung purposefully in his hand.

I sang out, "This won't save you, Cerise."

And then the blackjack hit me on the side of the head. I took it with a roll and surged into the guy. I hit him twice in the mid-section, and he went down, grunting. I trod on him as the other guy surged in for the kill. He clawed at me, an expert, aiming for the throat and then hitting low. I fought him off, but then the other guy came back. I went down in a flurry—a wave of blinding pain. Then I heard, as if from a long way off, Duke Cerise's voice, "Hold him up, boys. Hold him up against the wall."

I sagged against the wall and it wasn't all a fake, either.

They held me there.

Duke Cerise was right in front of me. "What did you want with Albanesi?"

"He's the mastermind."

Duke Cerise laughed. "You're wrong, Kent. I'm the man you want to worry over."

"Right now, I'm not worrying over anything." My lips were like pillows.

"You want to live?"

"Why not?"

"Okay, tell us all you know about Harbin."

It was my time to laugh.

Cerise's face went black. "Okay, Albanesi, get him back in that chair."

The big guy, middle-aged and paunchy, but husky the way he gripped me, hustled me into the chair. He grabbed at my shoulder blades, leaning down with his weight. He was grinning like he was looking forward to something real good.

I said thickly, "That's a nice daughter you got, Albanesi. You wouldn't want anything to happen to her, would you?"

The grin vanished. He turned his head quickly to where Duke Cerise stood, arms folded across his chest.

Cerise snapped, "Don't listen to him, you fool."

I said, "I thought you wanted me to talk."

Albanesi's mouth was set like a trap. "That's the wrong kind of talk, mister." He was still leaning over me, his hands resting lightly on my shoulders. Suddenly both his hands moved and I felt tingling pain shooting down the nerves of both shoulders. I must have writhed.

Albanesi said, "I'm fat, but a man doesn't have to be in condition when he knows what I know."

His hands moved off my shoulders and the pain went. His hands were caressing my neck. I felt his thumbs probing up behind my ears—and remembered the old commando trick used in modified form in the wrestling ring; the grip they call the "sleeper hold."

Then my blood started clamoring against my skull. Albanesi's face was hanging between me and the light like a huge moon in eclipse. In seconds, I knew, I wouldn't even be seeing his face.

Dimly I heard Cerise say, "Don't put him right out."

The grip eased. I felt my blood pounding as the interrupted flow went on.

Albanesi said, "What did Harbin tell you before he died?"

"Okay," I jerked out. "You asked for it." I struggled up in the chair. The room was very quiet. I said as convincingly as I could, "He told me all about the dope ring operating here in Havana. He told me who the principals were—he reckoned he'd taken the rap for the lot of you. He was plenty bitter about that."

I waited. Suddenly the silence was broken.

Cerise strode forward, pushed Albanesi aside and staring into my face snarled, "You're lying, Kent."

I stared right back at him. "Prove it."

He said, "Dan Harbin would never squeal on me!"

"It means a lot to you, huh? This new respectability of yours. It's a good front and you'd hate like hell to lose it. Right through you've been scared about what Harbin might have spilled before he checked out. I guess you were right to be scared. The jig's up, Cerise. No more fine front on Wall Street—no more membership to exclusive clubs—they don't have exclusive clubs in Sing Sing anymore."

He dived at me—I was waiting for it. I rolled sideways out of that chair and grabbed at Albanesi. I thrust at him, caught him off balance. He fell over Duke Cerise, who swore and then yelled something to the other two guys over by the wall. The next few seconds flicked by in a fast blur. Albanesi instinctively righted himself and plunged at me, hands outspread, as if going in for a judo kill.

If he'd stayed where he was he wouldn't have died.

A gun spat from one of the hoodlums by the wall. I dived at Cerise in that instant—and felt Albanesi crash into me with his shoulder. But he didn't grab me. The only move he made was toward the carpet, face first.

"By hell," said Cerise. "You got Albanesi!"

I looked at the hatchet men. They seemed frozen from shock. But Duke Cerise's hands were working, his face convulsed.

Thickly he said, "You've talked plenty, Kent. You just sighed your own death warrant." His head jerked round. "All right, boys, get him."

I guess nobody heard the door open, but four heads swung as one when Carol Weiler said from the doorway, "Are you going to kill me next, Duke Cerise?"

She took three paces into the room and stood there, tall, perfectly groomed, as poised as if she were walking into a ballroom, knowing she was the best-dressed, best-stacked, people's choice for the blonde of the year.

"Well, Duke?"

He said thickly, "Okay, boys, pack it up."

I glanced at the two hoods. They were putting away their guns nervously, as if they weren't sure of themselves any more.

Carol walked right up to me, glanced at me coldly, then inclined her head as she stared down at the body of Albanesi.

"Did you kill him, Duke?"

"Not me. No." Cerise hesitated. "It was an accident."

"Yes," said Carol. "It must have been a bad accident. Well, what are you waiting for? You're going to kill Kent and then me, aren't you?"

"You're talking like a fool." He was having difficulty framing the words, and I looked at him and saw the sweat on his face. Before that I'd known Duke Cerise had big aspirations to be an on-the-level guy with the very best people; now I knew for sure he was gone on Carol Weiler—maybe she started off as a convenient link between Cerise's organization and the all-powerful J. B. Weiler. But the way I read it, things had got out of hand. Cerise had fallen for the dame.

When she said nothing he jerked away abruptly. He snarled at the hoods. "All right, you guys, what you hanging around for? Get downstairs."

One of them took a step forward. "But, Duke—"

"You heard what I said. Go and wait for me in the car. It's parked in the alley. I'll be right down."

With a last glance at the honey-blonde, the two hoods walked to the door and went out quickly.

I fumbled for a cigarette. While I was lighting it, Duke Cerise said in a quick uncertain voice, "All right, Carol, let's show cards. This is between just us two. Never mind that punk detective."

I took the cigarette from my mouth. "Sure, go ahead. Don't mind me. I'm of age, and I guess I can take just about anything."

Carol turned her shoulder to me.

Cerise said, "Carol, baby. You've caught me flat-footed. I'm sorry about all this."

"Yes, I imagine you are," she replied. There was ice in her voice. "And as for showing cards—why, I think it's a showdown all round."

"You mean—?"

"Tonight, my father's agent Rock Alison stumbled into the Hotel of the Americas. He'd been shot in the shoulder. He'd lost a lot of blood and was in bad shape."

"Now see here, Carol, baby—"

"Yes," went on Carol remorselessly, "this is a showdown, Duke. For a long time I've known that you were behind the people who were blackmailing my father. Right through I made up my mind to get even with you and now—well, it looks as if the sands are running out."

I dragged on my cigarette, watching Duke Cerise take it. His face had gone a little pale, the sweat stood out on it. His hands were clenched at his sides.

At last he said, "So—you just played me along, eh?"

"You could say that," replied Carol coolly. "Things are going to be different from now—Rock Alison's been found."

"Yeah," I put in, "I guess that rates me a bonus from your old man."

For the first time in minutes she turned and looked at me full on.

"Are you feeling humble, Mr. Kent?"

"No," I said, "I wouldn't know how to."

I saw her flush.

I added, "It looks like I had you wrong, baby. Too bad about that. I sure hope the boyfriend's going to make out okay."

"To hell with you and your small talk," snarled Duke Cerise. He pulled a tiny .22 from an inside pocket. He jerked it toward me and then Carol. "The comic opera's over. Now I've come this far I might as well take somebody with me."

Before I could speak or move there came a heavy knocking on the door. A voice called in Spanish, "Police! Open up!"

7

Knives are nasty, Lolita ...

For a few moments nobody moved. Then Duke Cerise made a convulsive movement with his gun. He said thickly, "No crummy cops are going to take me in this town!"

For a moment I thought he was going to let me have it, but suddenly he dropped the .22 into his side pocket, turned and headed toward the far door.

The cops were banging on the other door, and as Cerise vanished I dived across the room, snapped back the latch—and in poured what seemed like twenty assorted cops. When they'd untangled themselves, I told them which way Cerise had gone. At a word from the young lieutenant, smart in his olive-green uniform, the gendarmes went out at a run.

That left us with the young lieutenant and—Rodriguez.

"Glad to see you," I told him.

"Who's this?" He nodded toward the body on the floor.

"I'd roll him over for you," I told him. "Only the lady's a little squeamish."

"After tonight," said Carol in a high strained voice, "I don't think I could be shocked by anything."

The lieutenant was on one knee beside the body. He looked round, and said something in Spanish. Rodriguez nodded and said to me, "Albanesi? I can't say he'll be mourned, in certain circles. Only maybe by his daughter."

I said, "How about Cerise?" I turned and headed for the door.

Rodriguez went after me, but by the time we hit street level, the uniformed cops were pouring back towards the entrance to the building. One of them talked rapidly with Rodriguez, who turned to me and said, "They got the other two gunmen, but Cerise got away. A car must have been parked down the side—"

"Yeah," I said. "Got a lead?"

"Sure. A police car's gone after him."

"Then it looks like we go after the police car."

Rodriguez looked at me then grinned. "All right, Larry. What are we waiting for?"

***

We had no difficulty picking up the red rear lights of the speeding police car. Rodriguez was at the wheel and as we took a corner fast he exclaimed, "Cerise must be crazy."

"I never met a grade-A mobster who wasn't."

"What in hell does he hope to achieve by running away?"

"Maybe more than by staying on his home base and taking the rap."

"Sure, sure," said Rodriguez impatiently. "But with his big connections, he stood a good chance of sliding out of most of the charges. After all—it's going to be hard to prove that he was the brain behind the Albanesi drug ring."

Nothing more was said until Rodriguez lessened the gap between us and the police car, then he ejaculated, "Looks like he's heading for the dock area!"

I sat up on my seat. "Cerise is nobody's fool. He was playing for big stakes and he'd have every loophole covered. What's to stop him making a getaway by water?"

"Old-fashioned," replied Rodriguez dryly, "but quite effective—that is if you have transport waiting for you."

"Cerise is the kind of guy who'd have everything waiting for him. Just in case of slip-ups—the quick way out."

"I think," said Rodriguez, "it's time we took over the lead."

He must have had his foot hard down. The car he was driving was a late model sedan with plenty power beneath its hood. We were practically airborne as he roared down the avenue. Traffic was light, and in no time we were abreast the police car, then passing it. As we went past Rodriguez gave three long blasts on the horn. After a moment the police car replied with another blast. I could hear sirens wailing from way behind and figured that the lieutenant had got busy with his own little posse. Cerise was making his last run in spectacular style. It was only a matter of moments before we picked up the rocking rear lights of his car. He was well clear of the downtown traffic, running through dockland streets, like silent canyons walled by warehouses and mercantile offices deep in shadow.

Rodriguez said, "He was staying at the Nacional Hotel. Too bad he didn't have time to collect his luggage."

I said, "Rodriguez, don't take him cheap."

He gave a snort and laughed. "You think I'm not trying, señor?"

"You're doing fine, only—that car Cerise is driving has got plenty of what it takes. What's more to the point, Cerise has got plenty, too."

"You're starting to worry me."

"Okay," I said. "Pass him and cut him off."

"Easier said than done." He broke off, jumped his foot off the accelerator as the car in front suddenly switched round a corner. Rodriguez had to fight the wheel to make it. He was in time to see Cerise swinging his auto off the sidewalk which he had climbed. Rodriguez let out his breath in a long whistle and said, "The guy's pushing it. What's more, he's heading for the pier. There's nothing surer."

We bucketed across an intersection and turned hard left, close behind Cerise, who didn't slow even for the red and green lights hanging over the port's railroad line.

Rodriguez exclaimed, "Heading for Havana Bay! I bet—" He stopped short and swung savagely on the wheel. There was a screech of tortured rubber as our car bounced and slid to a stop. Me, I was sitting on the edge of the seat like a rube at a Cinerama show. The air was filled with the clang of the shunting loco that had burst suddenly into view, almost like a trick shot in a movie; there was a wild clanging of bells and the red and green lights burning, steam wreathing about the big headlights, sparks spurting from the iron wheels as the loco churned to a stop squarely across the concrete pavement that led through to the pier.

And tangled right in the teeth of the loco were the remains of Cerise's car.

"Head on," said Rodriguez breathlessly, and added what seemed like a short prayer in Spanish.

"Too close for comfort," I said. My forehead felt suddenly moist. Then we were getting out of the car, running stiff legged toward the loco that loomed above us. There were other guys running and from some place way back some character was yelling.

But Duke Cerise wasn't yelling. What was left of him we found crumpled in the wreckage of his fine car.

***

Back in my hotel room I ran a shower, stripped off my shirt and went over to the phone and called room service.

"Send up a bottle of Scotch and some cracked ice."

I lit a cigarette and went to the window and looked out. For the first time since my arrival the lights of Havana seemed inviting and friendly. I was standing there, dragging on my cigarette, the sound of the running water in the background, when there came a knock at the door. I didn't turn my head.

"It's open!"

I heard the door click shut, then a voice said, "It's getting to be quite a habit."

I turned quickly.

Carol Weiler was standing there. There was a faint smile on her face.

I said, "Some day I'll make that shower." I added, "I figured you were the waiter. Stick around and I'll buy you a drink."

"I don't know that I want to drink with you."

I shrugged, reached for my shirt and was working my arms into it when Carol Weiler came up close and said, "I came to tell you a couple of things. One of them is that Rock booked himself into a room of his own here."

"I knew that. What's the other thing?"

"He's feeling much better and the doctor's hopeful that there'll be no permanent damage."

"You're talking like a book," I told her.

I saw her flush. "My conversation always seems to have a bad effect on you, Larry Kent."

"Yeah," I said. "Blame the climate. Excuse me," I added. "I think I hear my shower running away." I walked through to the annex and turned off the faucets. When I went back I found Carol had perched herself on the side of the bed and was thoughtfully lighting a cigarette.

I said, "Make yourself at home."

She said nothing.

There was a tap on the door and a waiter came in with Scotch.

"Put it right down there," I told him.

He glanced at me and then at the dame. He smirked.

I said, "On your way, buddy."

He went.

"Scotch?"

"Looks like I get no choice."

"Smart girl." I poured two drinks over the ice and carried them over to the bed. As I held out the drink, Carol slid off the bed and stood facing me. She made no attempt to take the glass.

"Don't you want to know what else I came for?"

"You tell me, baby?"

"I wanted to make you apologize for not believing me that other time."

"I guess everything's been straightened out now," I told her. "I had you wrong. Didn't you hear me apologize before?"

"Perhaps I'd like to hear you say it right out loud, slowly."

I put a hand under her chin.

She wrenched her head away.

I said, "I don't apologize to anyone."

She nodded, "I'd forgotten. It takes a real man to back down, doesn't it?"

"Say, what weight are you fighting at tonight?"

She said hotly, "You might at least have the decency to admit when you're in the wrong."

"Consider it admitted. Now, drink up your drink and we'll bury the hatchet, huh?"

She sighed stormily. "You know, Larry Kent, there are an awful lot of things about you that I detest."

"Tough."

"In fact, I'd be hard put to it to find anything about you that I really like."

"Maybe I lose a good night's sleep tonight."

"Can't you be serious about anything?" she blazed.

"Yeah," I said. "Every time I think about that bonus I'm going to collect from J. B. Weiler I get goose pimples. I figure I might take a vacation right here in Havana before I head home. With a bonus at the end of my trip—"

She broke in, "You think your work's all finished?"

"What else is there?" I took some of my drink. "Cerise is dead and so is Albanesi. They saved the U.S. quite a heap of money dying that way. Rodriguez and the police department are busy throwing the dragnet around the rest of Albanesi's ring. The rest, including Gus Elsinore, have headed out for pastures new. By tomorrow morning the only thing left of Duke Cerise will be a faint smell."

Carol said, "What do you intend to do about Rock?"

I stared at her. "What is there to do about that guy? A good guy, beaten up. He'll have to be shipped home just as soon as possible."

"He can fly out tomorrow, the doctor said."

"Great."

"Only he'll need somebody to go along with him."

"That shouldn't be hard to fix. With you around."

"Supposing I told you I didn't want to go back with him?"

"You need another drink."

"I haven't finished this one yet."

"Okay." I shrugged and finished my own and poured a fresh one.

Carol said, "I suppose I'd only be pandering to your conceit if I told you I'd rather stay in Havana with you."

Slowly I put my glass down on the table. Without looking at her I said, "Carol, did anyone ever tell you just how you work on a guy's nerves? I bet a hundred men have told you that already."

"Larry—"

"Yeah," I said. "You're the sort of dame that ought to be kept behind barbed wire. You're lethal, baby."

Suddenly she was close to me.

"Larry—"

"Don't do it, baby. Finish your drink and go right out there and forget all about this."

"Why should I? I don't want to forget. I want to stay here with you."

"You're nuts."

"I know I am and I hate myself for it, but—Larry, let me work on your nerves."

"You're doing a great job already, baby." I kept my hands at my sides. She was close to me, warm, pulsing. I said, "Break for recess."

"Larry—please." She grabbed at pulled my head down.

The next moment I felt an electric shock shoot from the back of my neck, clear down my spine. It was therapy plus.

I swung her away from me. Some of the blonde hair had slipped loose, veiling part of her face. Her lips were parted. I could see the white gleam of her teeth. Her eyes were like tempting pools.

Right then I didn't want to drown.

I said, "Rock Alison is one good guy. He needs you, baby."

"Please, Larry—" It was almost a choking whisper.

Her hands were out, fluttering.

I said, "I'm all through here, baby. When I get back to New York I'll collect my bonus. Let me know when the wedding is, I'll send you fish knives."

She swung her right hand and her palm cracked against the side of my face.

I stood very still. She sobbed and hurled herself at my chest. I let her hang there for a while and then put her aside, not ungently.

"You're a living doll," I told her. "Also, you're dynamite—in this climate." I tilted her head back and kissed her full on the mouth, then I pushed her away, turned her around and headed her for the door. "Don't forget that wedding invitation," I told her.

The door slammed.

***

I sat in the American Bar waiting for Lolita to show up.

She had disappeared right after the big raid on Albanesi's place. Me, I didn't put the cops wise when Lolita called me at the hotel. The way she was fixed, I figured there was no point in putting the finger on her for crimes that her old man had committed. And nothing would bring the past—and Jim Calloway—to life again. She was Albanesi's daughter, and she was Carol's friend and the trusted friend of J. B. Weiler.

And she was also the two-timer who had met Calloway in his early days at the Narcotics Bureau. It was because he had been crazy over her that he had sought her out when she returned to New York—and because he had found out too much about the set-up back of Harbin, he had been rubbed out.

A girl sat on the stool next to me. It wasn't Lolita. I glanced at her just in time to catch her own glance.

She smiled a little, without flushing, then turned to the bartender and ordered a Tom Collins.

I lit a cigarette and looked at her again. She had the reddest hair I'd seen in years—red, against a dead-white skin. There was a faint dusting of freckles over her short and perky nose. Her mouth was wide, and she wore the right kind of lipstick to go with that flaming hair.

She fumbled for cigarettes in her purse, dropped it and spilled the contents all over the floor. I stooped to help her pick up the mess. Our heads went down together. In that stooping position with our faces inches apart, I said, "Hi."

"Hi, handsome."

We straightened.

"You got everything there?"

"I think so," she said and busily stuffed the assorted articles back into her purse. "Thanks a lot."

"You're welcome," I told her. "How about a drink?"

"You mean to say you're unattached?" she said in a tone of mock surprise.

"For a little time," I told her. "I'm waiting for a dame."

She frowned—it was almost a scowl. "I don't like that line of talk."

"Tough." I waited until she'd finished her drink, then ordered a fresh one.

Then she thawed. "What's your name?"

"Larry."

"I'm Jane." She added quickly, "Please don't make any cracks about plain Jane will you? Back in Milwaukee where I come from, all the boys think it's a good opening line."

"They must have some smart guys around Milwaukee. What do you do there, beautiful? Model that ripe red hair?"

She laughed ... she was the kind of dame who moved everything when she laughed. It was some performance.

"Why, no I teach school in Milwaukee. This is my vacation and I'm spending it right here in Havana." She leaned towards me confidingly. "I came for a Cuban moon and romance and lots and lots of fun. Do you think I'll find it, Larry?"

"Keep looking," I told her.

There was a tap on my shoulder. It was a waiter.

"A lady wishes to see you in the lobby, Mr. Kent."

"Okay, I'll be right there." I turned to Jane, the girl from Milwaukee. "You staying here?"

"Why no, I'm at the Nacional."

"Living it up, huh?"

"I've been saving for years."

"See you around," I told her, flipped a hand and went out after the waiter.

Lolita was there wearing clothes for travelling—and the way she wore them she should have got a bonus from the travel agency.

"One million dollars," I told her. "Baby, you look terrific."

Her mouth was a sullen line. "You don't have to spray any compliments over me, Larry Kent. I want to talk to you."

"I've got a nice spot back there in the American Bar ..."

"No," she broke in. "I've got a car outside. Will you come?"

"Why not?" I followed her out the lobby, down the steps to the sidewalk. As we crossed it I took her by the arm and for a moment she yielded against me, then she stiffened and tore her arm away.

"Quit that, too," she snapped.

"Sure," I shrugged, opened the car door for her.

She slid in back of the wheel and I went round and got in the other side.

We drove in silence down the avenue and swung up toward the Morro Castle. Halfway up she took a side road and stopped in an avenue with thick trees growing either side. She cut the engine and turned to me.

"I've got something for you, Larry, on account of my father."

"I didn't kill him."

"Did I say you did? But you were there. I know why you were there. You're a skunk, Larry Kent. That's why I'm going to give you this."

I saw her right hand flash as it swept up from the purse in her lap. I'd been expecting something, but not a six-inch steel blade. I parried the blow, but felt the razor edge sear across my knuckles. Then I slapped down hard with my free hand and felt the knife strike my shoe. I slugged her in the throat and she fell back in the seat, whimpering.

"Lolita, that way you wind up in San Quentin."

"I hate you! Go to hell! You heel!" She cussed me out in Spanish. I let her finish, then lit two cigarettes and leaned over her and put one between her trembling lips. Then I took the knife and threw it out the car, grabbed her by the shoulders, slid her along the seat and crammed my way past her to the driving wheel. As I started up, Lolita sat forward, the cigarette glowing in her hand, "Larry? Please, Larry. Let me talk to you."

"Some other time."

"Please, I didn't mean to kill you—"

"If you had, it would have been tough."

"Please, Larry—"

"Yeah," I said. I drove down a block, swung into the main avenue. Then I said, "Tough about your old man. Tough about Jim Calloway, too. I guess he was a sap—we all are about dames. I've thrown away that torch I was toting for him. Now you throw yourself on to the first plane out of Cuba. Plenty of places to go to, Lolita. I guess your old man left you spare cash in dollars, pesitos and such."

"Stop for a moment, Larry, please."

I said, "I'll drop you at the bus station, Lolita."

"Damn you." Her hand was coming at me again.

I braked fast, brushed her to one side. She fell back in the seat, and the crumpled cigarette that she had jabbed at my face fell to the floor.

"Okay," I said. "This looks like it." I jerked the car to a standstill, opened the door and climbed out. Then I went round to her side and leaned on the door sill. She was slumped on the seat, her dark hair hanging lifelessly about her face.

"Nice knowing you, Lolita. Go some place and cool off, then write me, huh?"

She said nothing.

I could hear her crying.

I walked away from the car. I had to walk two blocks before I could hail a cab. I rode back to the hotel. In the taxi I wrapped a handkerchief around my knuckles. As I paid the hackie off he said, "Been in a fight, señor?"

"Yeah," I said. "She nearly won, too."

I could hear him laughing as I went up the steps.

I went into the American Bar. For a moment I thought she'd gone, but as I walked quickly over to the bar I saw her red head inclined toward a paunchy, bald-headed guy who was polishing his eye-glasses and laughing like he was having himself a ball.

I took the stool next to hers and ordered a Scotch. Then I leaned against her shoulder and said, "School's out, baby."

She swung round on her stool. Her mouth was a little open. Then she laughed.

"Why, hello! That was quick."

"Yeah," I said. "She broke the date."

"Too bad," cooed Jane. Her quick, greenish eyes noticed the bandage round my knuckles. "Did she bite you?"

"No, she used a knife."

She put back her head and laughed. Then she turned to the bald-headed, paunchy guy who was scowling on the stool next to hers.

"You hear that? This big guy went out with a girl and she used a knife on him. Or that's his story. It could only happen in Havana, couldn't it?"

The fat guy mumbled something and I said, "Tom Collins?"

Jane swung round again. "You're breaking something up, Larry."

"Tough," I said. "Finish your drink and we'll go find ourselves a moon."

Jane's green eyes were glowing like a cat's.

"Why not now?" she breathed.

"Later," I said.

ABOUT LARRY KENT

Larry Kent started his life as the hero of a half-hour radio show on Australia's Macquarie Network, and was inspired chiefly by the success of the hardboiled mysteries of Carter Brown. As the popularity of the radio show grew, the Cleveland Publishing Pty. Ltd decided to publish a series of Larry Kent novels. Two authors, Don Haring (an American who lived in Australia) and Des R Dunn (a Queenslander) are primarily associated with the series. Between 1954 and 1983, Larry appeared in well over 400 adventures.

Kent is a typical hardboiled private eye. He smokes Camels, drinks whisky and within the first dozen pages or so, has usually met a dame and is fighting for his life. His mean streets are pure New York (although the radio series was set in Australia) and include Harlem nightclubs and Jersey roadhouses.

Generally the body counts are high: about six deaths per novel.

But there's another side to Larry Kent. He's a Vietnam War veteran, he used to work for the CIA and still does, usually reluctantly, on occasion. And once, when an attempt was made on his life, the Agency paid for him to have plastic surgery that altered his appearance ... something he never quite managed to get used to.

Larry Kent is fast and fun, and Piccadilly Publishing is proud to be bringing his cases to a whole new generation of fans, complete with their original 'good girl' artwork.

These paperback editions are produced in cooperation with and by Bold Venture Press.

LARRY KENT, P.I. SERIES

Cry Twice, Kitten!
Honey-Blonde Blues
Go Go for Broke
The Heavenly Bodies
Witch Rhymes With ...
Call for a Corpse
Mourning Glory
Cry Blood, Baby!
The Key to Karen
The Skin Game
The Big Contract
Stripped to Kill
Bye Bye Benny
Crimson Lady
Sidewalk Empire
Spanish Harlem
Mona Lethal
Client: Mafia
Hello Dolly ... Goodbye
One More for the Road
Scorpio
Terror Below
The Weirdos
... And more to come!

Hardboiled fiction from Bold Venture Press ...

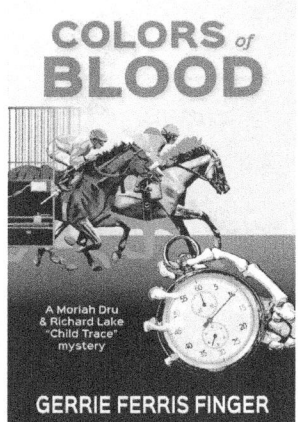

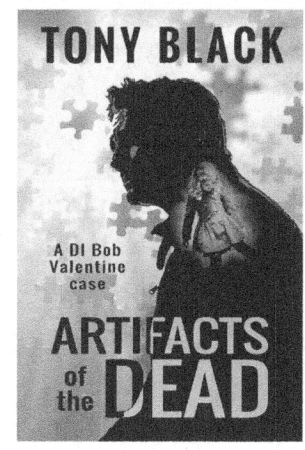

Colors of Blood
Gerrie Ferris Finger
The stakes are higher than ever when corruption surrounds a horsefarm preparing for Belmont and Saratoga.

Flying Blind
Howard Hammerman
A midlife crisis takes a turn for the worse when a pilot accepts a freelance assignment to save his plane from repossession.

Artifacts of the Dead
Tony Black
After a near-death experience, horrific visions guide DI Bob Valentine's hunt for a serial killer.

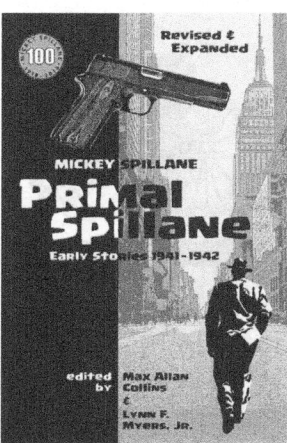

The Killers Are Coming
Jack Bludis
The Block — Baltimore's segregated area for vice can't contain the corruption, and P.I. Ken Sligo is about to uncork trouble.

Primal Spillane
Mickey Spillane
A collection of fast-paced stories, in a vareity of genres, by the creator of Mike Hammer, P.I.

Strictly Poison
Charles Boeckman
Pulp fiction fused with jazz — sleazy cops, bloated bigshots, and hen-pecked losers in stories by author/musician Boeckman.

www.boldventurepress.com

More from Bold Venture Press ...

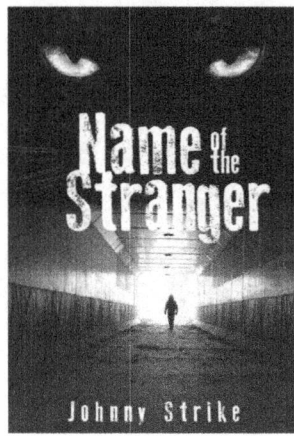

Hellbent On Homicide
Gary Lovisi
A refrigerator in a vacant lot wasn't empty — and detectives Griff and Fats hunt a serial killer making a contest of torture.

Name of the Stranger
Johnny Strike
A contemporary thriller of a mental patient demanding "closure" from his hapless, retired therapist.

No Torrent Like Greed
C.J. Henderson
A routine investigation into an ice cream company threatens everything Jack Hagee, P.I. holds dear.

Thubway Tham Meets the Crimson Clown
Johnston McCulley
Criminals face-off in a laugh-a-minute thriller from the creator of Zorro!

I'll Grind Their Bones
Theodore Roscoe
A reporter finds himself at the epicenter of murder for profit — and the prize is war between countries!

The Taxol Thief
Ceylon Barclay
When the USDA refuses to help, one man embarks on a desperate odyssey to save his wife from cancer.

www.boldventurepress.com

Three Golden Age heroes confront a diabolical force in the early days of World War II

Thrills! Suspense! Excitement!

TO BATTLE BEYOND

The Domino Lady, The Black Bat, and Inspector Lagrasse
An adventure of "The Originals" by C. J. Henderson

Made in the USA
Monee, IL
04 May 2025

16833510R00125